ONCE UPON WEST AFRICA

Enjoy a taste of Africa,

Phillip Martin

copyright © 2019 Phillip Martin

All rights reserved.

ISBN: 978-2-62249-466-8

Published by
The Educational Publisher Inc.
Biblio Publishing
BiblioPublishing.com
Columbus, Ohio

DEDICATED TO
DANIEL

Once Upon West Africa is a collection of fifty Liberian folk tales I collected as a Peace Corps Volunteer. These tales do not end with the words "and they all lived happily ever after." The tales from Liberia frequently taught a lesson where the evil, rotten, nasty person - usually that trickster Spider - gets it in the end. They are stories that deal with right and wrong, good and evil, justice and injustice. It's a rare story that has anyone living happily ever after - especially the one who needs to learn the lesson.

The Peace Corps is called the "Toughest Job You'll Ever Love." It was hard not to love the time I spent collecting African folk tales. I traveled across Liberia, eating and breathing a lot of red dust along the roadsides, to compile these stories. I wore out the bottom of my seat while riding in the back of crowded pickup trucks and also wore out my tape recorder in the process. In addition, I stayed in little villages, made new friends, connected with friends of friends and recorded stories at police checkpoints, in remote villages and under the starlight. I also had malaria four times and multiple motorcycle wrecks (some minor and a few major).

Over the years, I've edited, re-edited, added to and revised the tales. And, a year or so ago, I illustrated them as well. They've just been sitting around, gathering dust inside my computer and waiting to be discovered. Recently I met LeRoy Boikai in Columbus, Ohio, of all places. He couldn't believe the treasure I've been sitting on. Along with the Village Improvement Project, LeRoy wants these stories in the hands of the one and a half million students in Liberia. That's a big dream, bigger than I ever imagined. I believe he's going to make that happen.

It's been a long time since my Peace Corps days. I don't know what happened to most of my storytellers during the civil war. I probably never will. However, my best friend, Daniel, was a refugee in the Ivory Coast for several years before returning to the village in River Gee County where he was born. He has rebuilt his life there and serves as a local teacher and principal. I can't wait to give copies of this book to his students. These children are the hope and future of my Sweet Liberia.

PHILLIP MARTIN
Peace Corps Liberia
1988 - 1989

A VERY SPECIAL THANKS

I'd like to express a very special thanks to the many people involved in helping me to collect these folk tales.

Mark Ashley originally suggested that I write this book.
Kevin McGee allowed me to use his home - too often -
as I traveled back and forth across the dusty, red roads of Liberia.
Debbie Mattina and Amanda Thomas located tattered copies
of stories in Curriculum Centers from other parts
of the country and sent them in my direction.
Sara Strachar and Lori Olvez recorded stories on cassette from friends.
Pat Greendale and Paul Steinberg sent me stories that
some of their students had written.

But most of all,

a very special thanks to my Liberian friends
who spent hours telling me folk tales.
The list is incomplete because frequently total strangers told me stories.
However, I received a lot of help from:

Daniel Copeland, Joshua Dorbor, Kannah Dorbor,
James Forpoh, Isaac Golageah, Godwin Jlah, Albert Quayee,
Timothy Quejue, Thomas Sharpe, George Sown,
Fofana Tarbeh, Alphonso Salgbe Teah, Moses Toe, Amos Towah,
John Tweh, Garrison Waplo, Frederick Toe Warjolo, Moses Warjolo,
and George Williams.

And, finally,
grateful thanks to my editors with eagle eyes who made this
book a lot closer to perfection.

LeRoy Boikai, Beth Bond, Steve & Lyla Martin, Debbie Mattina,
Jennifer Mullen with Alana & Breana, and Pat Randolph

PREFACE

Village Improvement Project, Inc. is proud to collaborate with Phillip Martin in publishing these beautifully written and illustrated Liberian folk tales. I believe in this project so much that I personally took the time to read and edit the stories to conform to Liberian cultural norms. So, I can truly call this a labor of love and a project I sincerely value.

Village Improvement Project will ensure that this collection of 50 Liberian folk tales, a long overdue treasure missing in Liberian schools, is widely distributed throughout the Liberian school system and worldwide. There is an immediate need to provide culturally relevant reading materials for Liberian children to help build their foundational skills of reading and writing for academic success. The folk tales in this collection will not only help to preserve Liberian culture but will capture the imagination of young readers. They are stories that the children will want to read. And the more they read, the better their chances are for a brighter future.

Not only will these tales enhance the education and lives of Liberian students, but they will also help to spread Liberian culture around the globe. Librarians, teachers, and parents around the planet will share a little Liberian culture with their children as they learn about Spider, some African food, and tales from a culture they may not have ever otherwise known. Once again, everyone wins.

Dr. LeRoy Z. Boikai
President, Village Improvement Project, Inc.

TABLE OF CONTENTS

Chapter 1
1. The Paramount Chief Who Was No Fool — 1
2. The Bitter Ball Baby — 5
3. A Rogue in the Cassava Patch — 9
4. Share and Share Alike — 13
5. The Rat School — 17
6. The Wise Man Builds His House Upon the Rock — 21
7. Three Truths — 25

Chapter 2
8. Black Snake and the Eggs — 27
9. Spider and the Honey Tree — 31
10. The Beautiful Bride — 35
11. A Dirty Conversation — 39
12. A Friend in Time of Need — 43
13. A Grave Problem with Greed — 47
14. A Lesson in Manners — 51
15. A Scrambled Friendship — 55
16. Cat Dreams While Rat Schemes — 59
17. Free Ride? — 63
18. Musu, Bendu and Cinderella — 65
19. How Not to Make a Farm — 71
20. Man Forgives an Enemy and Finds a Friend — 75
21. Manjo and the Crocodile — 79
22. One Man's Trouble — 83
23. Sengbe and the Fishing Rules — 87
24. Sixteen Plums — 91
25. Spider's Smile — 95
26. Tale of Two Neighbors — 99
27. The Real Reason Spider Has a Small Waist — 103
28. The Sun's Daily Search — 109
29. The Tug of War — 113
30. Three Brothers with Bad Habits — 117
31. Turtle's Magic Rock — 123

Chapter 3

32. Beauty Is Only Skin Deep	127
33. Cockroach and Rooster	131
34. A Race to Remember	135
35. Bread for an Old Beggar	139
36. Cat Knows His Love Has Its Limits	143
37. Everyone Is Not Happy with Everyone	147
38. Home Sweet Boa's Home	151
39. Leopard's Burning Fear	155
40. Problem Solvers and Trouble Makers	157
41. The Farms of Tamba and Samba	161
42. The Mother Pot	165
43. The Palm Wine Trap	167
44. The Rule about the Moon and Stars	171
45. The Treasure Cave	175
46. A Gracious Host	179
47. Red Deer's Secret Mission	183
48. The House that Spider Built	187
49. The School Where Nothing Was Learned	189
50. Why Crocodiles and Humans Cannot Be Friends	193

Chapter 4
Deep in the Bush, Where People Rarely Ever Go
Three Plays

Spider and the Honey Tree	197
Black Snake and the Eggs	203
The Paramount Chief Who Was No Fool	210

Chapter 5
Liberian English Vocabulary Words — 220

CHAPTER 1

THE PARAMOUNT CHIEF WHO WAS NO FOOL

"Help me," the old man begged. "My neighbor has stolen from me."

The paramount chief gladly listened. It pleased him that others recognized his wisdom. "What exactly is the problem?" asked the chief.

"My neighbor stole my goats. I am too poor to replace them."

"And what do you have to say?" the chief asked the man's neighbor.

"I don't know what he is talking about," answered the neighbor. "I have many goats, but I have nothing that belongs to this man. No, I have not stolen any of this man's goats."

This would not be an easy problem to resolve. The paramount chief would have to rely on his wisdom. It was the kind of problem he enjoyed the most.

"I have a test for you," announced the chief. "Whoever passes the test will own the goats. Go home until you can answer this for me. I want to know what the fastest thing in the world is. Do not return until you have my answer."

The two men left shaking their heads. Who could answer that question? Was it the cheetah? Perhaps it was the eagle that soared above in the sky. Who knew the correct answer?

The old man repeated the question to his daughter, Ziah. She was as beautiful as she was wise. Right away, she whispered the answer that would please the chief. The old man returned to the chief the following morning.

The chief was certainly surprised. "You already have the answer?"

"Yes," replied the old man, "it was not difficult."

"And, what is the fastest thing in the world?"

"Time," said the old man. "We never have enough of it. It always goes too fast. There is never enough time to do all that we want to do."

The answer amazed the paramount chief. He wasn't sure if he could have answered the question as well. "Who helped you? Who gave you these words?" demanded the chief.

"They are my own words, my own thoughts," lied the old man. "There is no one else who helped me."

"If you are not telling the truth, I will punish you," warned the chief. "You will never forget the day you lied to me."

The old man was too afraid to continue the lie. "It was my daughter, Ziah, who gave me the words," he confessed. "She is a very wise woman."

"She must be!" thought the chief. "I would like to meet her."

Not long after that, the old man presented his daughter Ziah to the paramount chief. If the chief was amazed at her wisdom, he was captivated by her beauty. "You are indeed a wise and lovely woman. I would be honored to have you as my wife. Will you marry me?"

"The honor is mine," Ziah said with a smile.

Although the chief was pleased, he was also concerned about having such a wise wife. He did not want her to interfere with the problems brought before him. He didn't want to share this honor with anyone, not even his wife.

"Everything in my house is yours," declared the chief. "I only have one rule for you. You must never involve yourself with the problems brought before me. This is your only warning. If you break this rule, I will send you from my house."

The chief's new wife only smiled at his command.

Things went well for quite some time. The paramount chief continued to hear people's problems while Ziah kept herself busy without becoming involved. Usually, she agreed with his decisions. Always, she kept quiet about what her husband said . . . until the day she didn't!

One day, the chief gave one of his puzzles to two shepherd boys who argued over a sheep. The real shepherd wandered into the chief's garden and spoke aloud to himself, not knowing that Ziah was there and could hear him. So, Ziah knew who was the real owner of the sheep. She also knew that she shouldn't help the boy. It was her only rule. But he was so upset!

"Tell me about this puzzle my husband gave you."

"The chief asked for the impossible," he sighed. "He gave us each an egg and said that whoever could hatch the egg by tomorrow would own the sheep."

"Young shepherd, the solution is so obvious," declared Ziah. "Take some rice to the chief. Tell him to plant it today so that in the morning you will have rice to feed your chicken. He will know that it is just as impossible to grow rice in one day as it is to hatch an egg that quickly."

"Yes, I can do that!" cried the boy.

"But remember this, my shepherd, you cannot tell the chief that I helped you. You must keep that our secret."

"You can trust me!" the boy replied, as he ran to the chief with the rice. He said exactly the words he was told. However, the chief was not impressed; he was angry! "Who told you this? Who gave you the rice?" he ordered. "These words are too wise for one so young."

"They are my own words, my own thoughts," said the boy, too afraid to speak the truth. "There is no one else who helped me."

"If you are not speaking the truth, I will punish you," warned the chief. "You will never forget the day you lied to me."

The boy was too afraid to continue the lie. "It was Ziah!" he cried. "She knew you'd understand the wisdom."

The chief understood his wife's wisdom and gave the sheep to the young shepherd. But, he was furious that his wife had broken his only rule. He called her before him and scolded, "Didn't you know all that I have is yours? You live here with me and I only had one rule for you. And, you have broken that rule. I warned you. Now, go back to your father's home."

"Before I leave, may I fix you one final meal?" asked the woman. "Then, I will take what is mine and go."

"Yes," answered the chief. "Make whatever you want. Take whatever you want. Just be sure that you do not remain here tonight!"

Now, Ziah knew how to cook very well. Her palm butter and beans gravy were delicious. But, she knew the chief's favorite dish and she prepared cassava leaves on this special occasion. And, of course, she served it with a generous amount of palm wine. Before the meal was finished, the chief became very drunk and quietly fell asleep. Ziah smiled because everything worked exactly as she had planned.

With her family's help, she carried the sleeping paramount chief to her father's home. They placed him on a bed, and he slept soundly through the night. But, in the morning, the chief's voice boomed throughout the house. "Where am I? What am I doing here?" he demanded.

Ziah entered the room and grinned.

"I asked you what am I doing here!" repeated the chief.

"You said I could take whatever I wanted from your house. I wanted you, and so I took you."

The chief had to smile when he heard that. "You are certainly a wise woman," he replied. "Come return with me to our home. Only a fool would send away such a woman."

"And you, my chief, are no fool," whispered the clever wife.

THE BITTER BALL BABY

In a tiny village deep in the center of the bush, there once lived an old woman named Fatu. She lived alone in a small mud hut, but it was never empty. Fatu's home was the center of village life. She was everyone's grandmother. Her home was where all the children came to play. They adored her! Her front porch was where the village women came to prepare supper. It was also where the men came to look when they couldn't find their wives and children at home.

Fatu's home was never quiet. Women shared stories on her porch. Children giggled and laughed in her yard. Goats played in her backyard pen. Men often stopped to see if there might be some extra bitter ball soup and rice. There was plenty of noise, laughter and love. But Fatu kept one secret that she never told any of her friends. She just couldn't tell anyone how very unhappy she really was.

Only one thing could make Fatu happy. Only one wish would change her life. And, that one wish would someday come true. Fatu was sure of it. One day she would have a child of her own.

Every day Fatu prayed for this child. She never gave up this hope. Each morning, she searched the area around her home. She wanted to see if the genies had given her a son. Each day, as she walked to her farm, she looked along the path. Maybe her daughter might be there? Each night, she expected to see a baby when she opened the door to her hut. One day she knew her prayers would be heard.

As Fatu awoke one morning, she sensed something was different. She felt the twinkle of magic in the air. "This might be the day!" she whispered. "Maybe I will finally find a child today!"

Fatu quickly said her prayer for a child and then ran to the window. She looked in her yard, but she found no son. The old woman wrapped herself into her lappa dress and searched around the house for a daughter. She looked in the rice bin, under the bed and even in the goat pen. She did not find a child. But hope remained. Fatu believed in the power of the genies. The magic she felt in the air had to come from them.

There was no time for breakfast that morning. Fatu had to get to the farm. Maybe there would be a daughter waiting for her along the roadside? She hardly noticed when her friends said hello. Her eyes scanned the sides of the dusty road looking for a child.

Fatu's heart nearly broke by the time she arrived at her farm without a baby. She busied herself with work. There was plenty to be done in the garden. The cassava needed the weeds pulled, and some of the bitter balls were ripe enough to pick.

At the end of her long day of work at the farm, Fatu placed a basket of bitter balls on her head and slowly started her long walk home. "I better look closely along the side of the road this time," she thought. "Something magical could happen, and I don't want to miss it."

The walk home took much longer than usual. Fatu searched behind each giant bug-a-bug hill along the roadside. She looked deeply into the growth of bamboo in the forest. She listened carefully for a child's cries at each clearing. No matter how hard she looked, there was no child to be found.

"How long do I have to wait?" cried Fatu. "It just doesn't seem fair. I thought there was magic in the air today. I thought this would be the day my prayers would be answered."

It was well after dark by the time Fatu reached her home. She saw the lights of her neighbors' cooking fires long before she reached the village. She smelled the smoke mixed with palm oil and spices as she neared her hut. The children played in the next hut while the youngest one cried. Fatu ignored all of this. Her mind only had one thought. "I cannot wait forever."

Fatu placed her basket of bitter balls on the porch and reached to open the door. The hut was unusually quiet, and again Fatu noticed a hint of magic in the air. As the old woman stepped inside, she felt magic swirl through the room. The room lit up like the sun. The light blinded her for a moment. When she was finally able to see, Fatu couldn't believe what she saw. A genie stood before her!

"Who are you?" cried Fatu.

"Don't be afraid, Fatu. I can't believe you don't know me. I am the genie you have prayed to for so long."

"W-w-what do you want? Why are you here?" asked Fatu.

"Weren't you expecting me, Fatu?" said the genie. "I have something just for you."

"You mean my time has come to finally have a child?" asked Fatu.

"Yes, Fatu, you have been such a patient and loving person. It is time for you to have your own child. You must only tell me if you want a boy or a girl."

"A girl!" cried Fatu. "I would love to have my own little girl!"

The genie smiled and said, "Go get one of your bitter balls and roll it towards me."

Fatu quickly ran back to the porch where she left the basket. She grabbed the largest bitter ball from the top and rolled it to the genie. It bounced off his foot and changed into a beautiful daughter. Fatu squealed with delight as she raised the baby in her arms. She was so happy that she almost didn't hear the genie's warning, "Do not ever let the child hear the words 'bitter ball' come from your mouth. Remember this warning because I will only tell it to you this one time."

And with that, the genie disappeared as quickly as he had appeared. Fatu didn't have a chance to thank him, but he could see it in her smile and hear it in her laughter.

Baby Hawa changed Fatu's life. Her hut was busier than ever. The neighborhood children visited more often and stayed even longer. They loved to play with Hawa. The village women all shared tips on how to best take care of the child. Even the village men had to take turns carrying the baby.

It was difficult for Fatu and her neighbors not to spoil Hawa. As the child grew, Fatu tried to provide her with all that she could. Hawa helped her mother clean house, gather firewood, wash clothes and draw water from the stream. Usually, she did this cheerfully. But there were times when she felt lazy and complained about the daily chores.

One day, when Hawa was much older, Fatu had an errand for her.

"I need you to go down to the market and buy me some peppers," said Fatu.

"Oh, Mother," Hawa moaned, "I'm too tired to go to the market. I want to go play with my friends."

"If you are not too tired to play, then you are not too tired to go to the market," replied her mother.

Hawa refused to listen. She dashed out the door and ran down the path away from the market.

Of course, that really vexed her mother. She raced to the door and cried out, "Come back here! You're acting like a lazy bitter ball!"

Suddenly, the racing daughter changed back into a rolling bitter ball. A boy playing on the path kicked it like a football into the bush. In tears, poor old Fatu realized that she must be careful what she says in anger. Unfortunately, she learned this lesson too late.

A ROGUE IN THE CASSAVA PATCH

"Rogue! Rogue! Rogue!" cried Red Deer. "There has been a rogue in my bitter ball patch."

"Help me!" called Turtle. "I have also been rogued. The rogue took some of my rice."

"Two rogues in one day," observed Leopard. "This is not good. Last week a rogue stole beans from Monkey and palm nuts from Dog. We must catch this rogue."

"How can we catch someone so clever?" asked Red Deer. "Nobody has seen him do anything."

"He isn't the only clever one around here," said Leopard. "We must set a trap, a trap with tar in the shape of a human being. The rogue has not yet come to take any of my cassava. So, this is where we will catch him. Yes, I will place the trap on my farm."

"But what happens if the rogue goes to another farm instead of yours?" asked Turtle.

"I'm sure he will come to my farm," Leopard said with an assured smile. "I want you to tell everyone that my farm has the biggest, the most incredible, the most wonderful cassava that you have ever seen. Yes, if you spread the word to everyone, the rogue will hear it. I'm sure the rogue will come to my farm."

So, that is exactly what Turtle and Red Deer did. They set out to tell everyone near and far about the cassava at Leopard's farm. While they did that, Leopard created his trap with tar. He shaped it like a human being and placed it along the edge of his cassava patch.

Of course, the rogue heard the news.

And, of course, he made plans to come to Leopard's farm that night to steal some of that incredible cassava.

After midnight, the thief crept into the farm. As he began digging the cassava, he noticed a "human being" nearby standing just at the edge of the patch.

"Who's there?" asked the rogue. "Why are you out here so late at night? Do you think I am a rogue? Well, that just isn't true at all. No, no, no. I am not a rogue. Nothing like that. I just want to see the huge cassava for myself."

The "human being" said nothing.

The rogue said, "Come on over here and join me. I'm sure you would like to see this cassava, too. Isn't that right?"

Again, the "human being" said nothing.

That silence really bothered the rogue.

"Can't you talk?" asked the rogue. "What's the matter with you? You are a rude human being. Talk to me! It is not polite to refuse to answer my questions when I talk to you."

More silence.

And, still, even more silence.

The rogue didn't appreciate it one little bit. "What's the matter with you? Talk to me!" He was so vexed that he marched over and hit the "human being" with his fist. And, much to his surprise, his hand stuck to the tar.

"What's this? Let me go!" demanded the rogue. "Let me go this very instant!"

But, the "human being" still said nothing.

And, he didn't let go of the rogue.

This was too much for the rogue. "If you don't let go of me, I'm going to kick you!" And, that's just what he did. He kicked the "human being" with his foot as hard as he could. And, it also stuck to the tar! The harder the rogue fought, the more trapped he became.

"Let go of me! Let me go right now!"

But, the "human being" never let go of the rogue. The two fought all night long. The "human being" never tired and he never once let go of the rogue.

In the morning, Turtle, Red Deer and Leopard came to the cassava patch. And, that's when they learned the identity of the rogue.

"Spider! So you are the rogue!" cried all three animals.

"Oh, no, you are mistaken. I am not the rogue," replied Spider. "The rogue is this human being. I caught him here last night as I sat guarding your cassava harvest."

"You cannot fool us, Spider. That 'human being' is a trap I made to catch the rogue," replied Leopard. "And, it caught a rogue. You are that rogue, Spider."

"Yes, and we caught you red-handed," snapped the turtle.

"It's more like black, sticky tar-handed," Red Deer giggled.

"Well, we have our rogue, and we know what to do with him," declared Leopard.

The animals really did know what to do. They took Spider to town and told everyone they saw exactly who their rogue was. And, the citizens knew exactly what to do. They beat Spider. Yes, every single person in the town had their chance to teach that rogue a lesson he would never forget. For you see, there was no way for Spider to escape the beating because the "human being" still would not let go of him.

Spider didn't live happily ever after but the local farmers were much happier for quite some time.

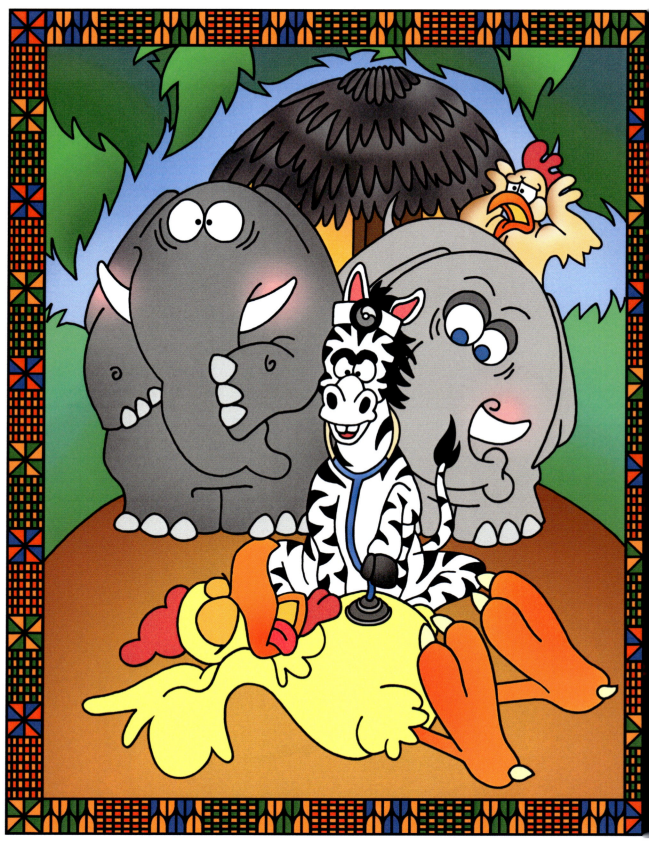

SHARE AND SHARE ALIKE

"We've worked hard on our farm this year," said Elephant. "I'm very pleased with our efforts."

"Yes, I agree with you, my friend. We certainly have worked hard," said Bush Chicken. "We have enough rice for both of us and will even have some rice to sell in the market."

"I know what we should do with that extra money. Let's buy ourselves a cow," suggested Elephant.

"The meat will be so sweet!" Bush Chicken agreed. "It's a wonderful idea, my friend."

So, that's exactly what the two friends did. They bought themselves a cow. Naturally, it was understood that they each were to take home equal shares of the meat. Well, at least, that was Bush Chicken's understanding.

"Bush Chicken, my good friend," said Elephant, "I am not sure if you know that my father's head is hurting. Please let me take the cow's head to make a special soup for him. I am sure it will make him feel so much better."

"I have no problem with that, my friend. Yes, take the head home for your father," said Bush Chicken. "And as for me, I think that I will have some of the . . . "

But Elephant interrupted his friend one more time. "And, Bush Chicken, have I told you that my mother's legs are bad? Please, I'm begging you, let me take the cow's legs home to prepare a special dish for her."

"Go ahead, my friend, I think that you should take the legs home to your mother," agreed Bush Chicken. "So, now, I think that I will select for myself the ... "

And once again, Elephant interrupted his friend. "Do you happen to know about my brother, Bush Chicken? I'm so sorry to tell you that he has a bad heart. Please let me take the heart for my brother."

"I had no idea that your family was so sick. Yes, you should take the heart for your brother," said Bush Chicken. "So, now tell me, how is your sister's health?"

"I'm so very glad that you asked about her. She has a bad liver. Bush Chicken, my dearest friend, will you please let me take the liver for her?"

"Yes, of course, you may take the liver for your sister," replied Bush Chicken.

But there were more problems in Elephant's family. Eventually, he also asked for the kidneys, the lungs, the back, the tail, and every other big piece of meat from the cow. When he finished, there were only a few small parts left for Bush Chicken to keep. Elephant happily returned to his family with almost all of the meat from the cow. Everyone was extremely happy about the food and so very pleased that Elephant had tricked Bush Chicken out of so much good meat.

As for Bush Chicken, she took her small portion of the meat home. Then, she roasted up the tiniest amount of it. When she tasted only a nibble, she let out the most terrible scream. Everyone heard it, and a few of the neighbors saw her as the chicken flew up in the air and fell to the ground still screaming. All of her friends ran to see what was the matter, including Elephant. "What's wrong?" he asked. "Are you sick? What's the matter with you?"

"It's that meat!" screamed Bush Chicken. "Do not eat the meat. Don't let anyone in your family touch it. The meat is poisoned!"

"POISONED!" cried Elephant.

"That's right, my friend."

"Oh, no! I must get the meat from all of my family. Please excuse me." Elephant raced home and gathered all of the meat from his family, very thankful that none of them had yet eaten any. As he carried the meat into the bush to bury it, he saw his friend, Bush Chicken, standing on the path before him.

"Thank you for saving my family, Bush Chicken," said Elephant. "I hope you are not too sick."

"No, I am not sick at all," declared Bush Chicken, "but I am very vexed!"

"Vexed? Why are you vexed?"

"You should know very well why I am vexed!" scolded Bush Chicken. "We worked together to make the farm. Am I right?"

"Yes," agreed the elephant.

"And, we worked together to take care of the rice. Is that correct?"

"Yes, again," said the elephant.

"And, together we harvested the crops. Is that right, Elephant?"

"Of course, it is," he nodded.

"Then, how could you try to take all of the good parts of the meat for yourself? I lied when I said the meat was poisoned."

"You lied?"

"Yes, the meat is not bad. It is YOU who are bad!" clucked Bush Chicken.

Elephant knew his friend was right. He was ashamed when he realized the full truth of what he had done. "Let's divide the meat one more time. This time it will be divided fairly. And, you may be the first one to make a selection, my friend. Yes, take the very best part of the meat for yourself."

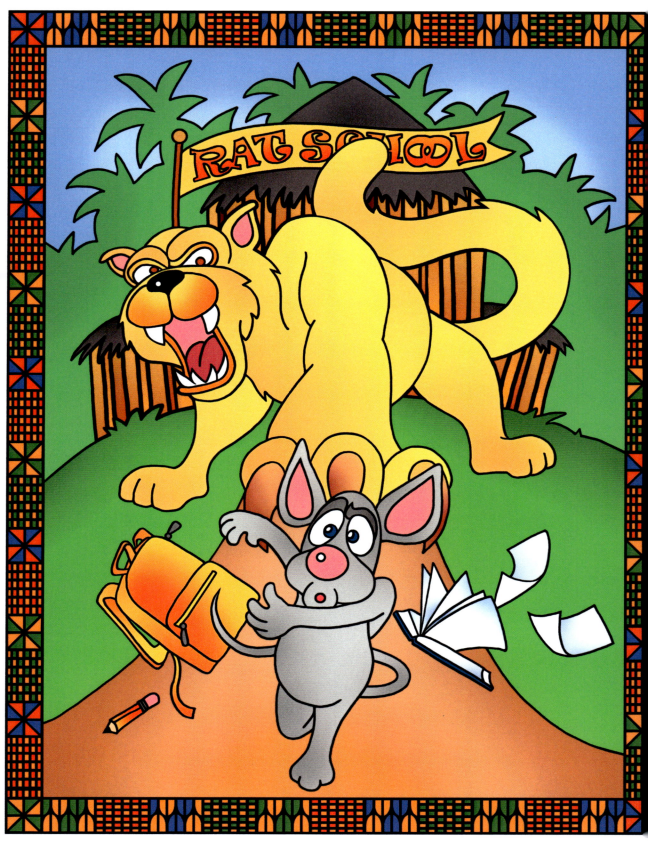

THE RAT SCHOOL

"I am very concerned about the rats who are living in our village," explained Cat to the chief. "They don't have a school, and this is not good at all."

"I agree with you. What do you suggest we do about the problem?" asked the chief.

Cat looked at the old elephant and declared, "You know that I am a teacher. I think I should start a rat school in our community. I could teach them many things."

"A school is an excellent idea," agreed the chief. "I would also like to come to this school."

"Oh, no, my chief, you are too old and much too wise to go to any school," said Cat. "No, I think that this community school should only be for the rats."

Actually, Cat didn't care about the rats at all. No, not one little bit. This school was just a clever plan of his to capture the rats in the village. If Cat could eat all of the rats that came to his school, he would not need to make a farm. And, he didn't like to work on a farm. Yes, the cat thought the school was a very good - and delicious - idea.

The rats, not knowing it was a trap, were delighted when the chief announced Cat would open a school for them. Everyone agreed it was so very kind of Cat to make such a generous offer. Cat just smiled when he heard this praise. He said it was his pleasure to taste . . . er . . . teach all of them.

"Registration for school begins tomorrow," said the cat. "There are many tests that I need to give my students so I can only register one rat each day. I will look for the first rat tomorrow morning at eight o'clock sharp."

Early the next morning, the very first rat proudly walked out of town to the school compound that Cat built. As Cat welcomed his first student, he quickly locked the door behind him. Then, he ushered the rat into the classroom.

"Where are all the books? Where are the desks?" asked the rat. "Where is the chalkboard?"

"There are no books or desks. There are no papers or chalk."

"I've never heard of a school without these supplies," declared the rat. "What kind of school is this?"

"Didn't I tell you, little student?" replied Cat with a smile. "It is a cooking school."

"Cooking school? Why did you create a cooking school? What are we going to cook?"

"RATS!" shouted the cat as he grabbed his first student.

The cooking lesson for the first day of Rat School was soon over. Cat licked his lips and happily waited for day two of registration. It was such a delicious plan. And, it was so very successful.

Registration at Rat School continued for several weeks, and there was so much interest in the project. Many of the villagers asked Cat how his school was going. He assured them that all of his students were hard at work. There was so much learning taking place at the school. Only a few of the villagers noticed Cat gaining any weight.

Small Rat was a little suspicious when it was finally his day to register at school. He was tiny, but he was not at all foolish. As far as he was concerned, Cat was mysteriously too fat.

"Welcome to Rat School," greeted the teacher. "It is good to see you, Small Rat. Come on in."

"Why don't I hear any of the other students in your school?" asked Small Rat.

"Oh, my friend, they are busy studying."

"And can you tell me why they don't ever come to the village on weekends?"

"That just isn't possible, Small Rat. There is always too much to learn here."

"Well, I really want to see my cousin, Big Rat, before I come to the school."

"That just isn't possible. You see, your cousin is too busy with his studies."

"Then I don't think that I will register for school. Honestly, I do not want to study that much," said the rat.

Cat could tell this student was suspicious about what was happening at his school. And, he certainly couldn't let the rat go back to the village and spread his fears. There were still too many rats to eat. Besides, it was too late in the season to start his farm.

The teacher knew he must act quickly.

He urged Small Rat a little closer to the door. The student peeked around the corner. He saw a few scattered ribbons that his friends had worn when they came to school to register. He knew his friends would never throw their ribbons aside like that. That was when Small Rat knew for certain that the school was actually a trap.

He turned and ran!

Cat pounced after him, but Small Rat was just too clever in the bush. He turned left, then right and ran in a few circles. Cat could simply not catch him. Small Rat raced back to the village and spread the word about the school to all of his friends. The school was closed forever and the hunger season was very, very long for the unemployed teacher.

THE WISE MAN BUILDS HIS HOUSE UPON THE ROCK

One day as Spider climbed up a mountain high in the bush, he found one of his friends sitting on a huge rock. "My friend, what are you doing here? I see you have sticks, thatch and a cutlass. What do you plan to do with these materials?"

"Isn't it obvious?" replied the man. "I plan to build a house."

Now Spider found this to be very strange. This man was well known for his wisdom, yet he was doing a very foolish thing. No one could build a house on this rock. It was too hard to make holes for the support posts. There was no mud nearby for plastering the walls. The strong winds on the mountain would certainly blow the house down. Spider explained the problems to his friend, but the man smiled as if he already knew all of these things.

"Here, have some palm wine and enjoy the view with me," the man said with a smile. "From this mountain, you can see along the river and on to the village beyond. You must admit, it is a lovely view from here."

"Lovely, yes," admitted the spider, "but not very smart! I still don't understand this at all. You picked a foolish place to build a house and brought all the materials here, but it's obvious you haven't done any work. What's going on here? Are you crazy?"

"No, my friend," replied the man, "I am not crazy at all. I know exactly what I am doing. I haven't told you the whole story. Do you see the large house down there in the village? There is a woman living there who has a beautiful daughter that I plan to marry."

"I know that woman," interrupted Spider. "That woman won't let anyone marry her daughter!"

"I know that, but I really enjoy the challenge. For the past several months, I have brought the woman lappas, country cloth, corn, chickens and meat. Finally, she said I could marry her daughter if I build a house on this rock."

"But that's not possible!" cried the spider. "The old woman knows that and is just using it as another way to prevent the marriage of her daughter."

"We'll see about that," replied the man. "Here comes the woman with some food for me. Now, go hide in the bush and listen. I don't want her to see you and think I wasn't working."

Spider hid just as the woman came up the path to the big rock. She observed the work site and frowned. "It doesn't look like you've done any work here."

"I've been very busy here, Mother. Thank you for this food. Ah, it's the crabs and rice that I requested. You are too kind to me, Mother."

"Don't call me 'Mother' until after you've married my daughter."

"Yes, Mother."

"Have you done any work here? You don't even have one pole ready. You aren't very serious about this work."

The man didn't say anything. He just ate the rice. When he had eaten enough to satisfy his hunger, he bit down on one of the crabs. "Ouch!" he cried out. "These crabs are too hard. I think I might have broken a tooth. Don't you know how to prepare crabs properly?"

The woman was very embarrassed. She took the soup back down the mountain and promised to return after she had boiled the crabs longer. "I'll return with a soup you will enjoy," she promised.

Spider and the man watched the old woman climb down the mountain. It was a long walk, and she appeared to be tired upon arriving at her home.

Her lovely daughter rushed out to greet her.

"Look how she wears her hair," admired the man with a smile. "She will make a lovely bride."

"If that mother ever agrees to the wedding . . . " added Spider.

Several hours later, the woman made the same climb back up the mountain for the second try with her crab soup. It smelled wonderful. The man greeted her warmly as she approached the rock.

"Thank you, Mother. You've been working hard today."

"Never mind that. Here's your soup. Eat it now and do not call me 'Mother'!"

"Yes, Mother."

But, when the man bit into a crab, it was still too hard to eat. The woman didn't believe it until the man took a palm nut and struck a crab. The palm nut, not the crab, broke.

"You are making an old woman out of me," muttered the mother. "Give me the crabs. I will boil them one more time."

As soon as the woman left, Spider came out of hiding and said, "She's about ready to boil you, my friend."

The two friends enjoyed more palm wine while the woman went back down the mountain. They talked and laughed as they watched her build a huge fire. She boiled the crabs several more hours because she was very determined to make a soup this man could eat.

It was nearly sunset when the woman made her final trip back up the mountain. She shoved the pot in front of the man and declared, "Here's your soup!"

"Thank you, Mother. I am very hungry."

"Just eat your soup and DO NOT CALL ME 'MOTHER'!" she screamed.

"I'm sorry, Mother," said the man, "but I still cannot eat these. Do you think I can eat something as hard as rocks? It would break my teeth to eat these crabs."

The old woman was vexed. It had been a hard day for her and what patience she possessed was long gone. She grabbed the pot of soup and threw it down the side of the mountain. She cried, "These crabs will never be soft. They are too hard. I can never cook them."

"And I am unable to build a house on this rock because it is too hard," replied the man with a grin.

Instantly, the old woman saw the wisdom of the man's words. She turned to go down the path. Just before she disappeared from sight, she said, "You are wiser than all the rest who have wanted to marry my daughter. You may have her as your bride."

The man was very pleased with his victory. As their celebration began, the man whispered in his friend's ear, "I must tell you one secret. I never liked crab soup."

Spider laughed with the man and assured him, "Today you have nothing to crab about."

THREE TRUTHS

Leopard purred to himself as he relaxed along the stream. "I can't remember when the breeze was so fresh, the water so cool and my belly so full. It's just a good day to be alive," he thought.

The stream was one of the few still flowing during the long dry season. Every day the animals of the bush came to refresh themselves with the cool water. This day was no exception for Red Deer. She came to the edge of the water with no idea that Leopard was near. Red Deer bent her head down low to take in a long drink. It was just what she needed on such a hot afternoon. When she finished her drink, she raised her head. Only then did she notice Leopard watching her from his perch on a big rock.

"What do I do now?" she wondered. "If I try to run, Leopard will certainly catch me. The only way to escape is to use my head. I am more clever than any leopard."

Leopard just licked his lips and grinned at Red Deer. "How good to see you today. I must say you're looking very delicious."

"It's good to see you too," lied Red Deer. "I haven't seen you for a long time. I do hope all is well with you."

"There is no need to lie to me," said Leopard. "I won't eat you today if you can tell me three truths that everyone would believe."

Red Deer was so nervous she could hardly think at all. Finally, she came up with one idea that she felt to be a truth. "Leopard," she began, "if I had known that you were at this stream just now, I would not have come here."

"I believe that to be the truth," agreed Leopard. "Now, what is your second truth?"

"If you don't eat me and I go back to the village, nobody will ever believe that I really saw you at the stream."

"I know that to be true, too," replied the leopard with a smile. "Everyone knows I love the taste of deer meat."

"And the last truth," declared the deer, "is that you are not very hungry right now. If you were hungry, you would have already eaten me."

"You are a wise deer," said Leopard. "You told me three truths. I cannot lie to you. Go on back to your village. I will not eat you today."

Red Deer scampered away from the stream before Leopard changed his mind. She shook her head in disbelief. "I told the truth three times today, but if I speak the truth at my village, everyone will say I am a liar."

CHAPTER 2

BLACK SNAKE AND THE EGGS

"My eggs!" cried Chicken. "One of my eggs is missing! Yesterday I had twelve eggs, and today there are only eleven."

As Chicken fled her nest to find Rooster, she had no idea that she was about to lose even more of her eggs. Just out of view of the nest, the thief patiently waited for Chicken to leave her eggs again. Black Snake crept slowly and quietly up to the nest. He eyed the eggs and quickly swallowed one.

Black Snake smiled to himself. His plan had been so simple and had worked so well. Quickly and silently, he swallowed another egg. It slid far down his long throat before his muscles crushed the fragile shell. "I'll be back later for another delicious egg, my little chicken," hissed Black Snake as he slithered away. "Thank you for another fine meal. It has been a pleasure."

Meanwhile, the frantic chicken led Rooster back to her nest. "Why would someone take one of my eggs?" she clucked. "I just don't understand this at all!"

"Are you sure you counted correctly? Maybe you just thought you saw eleven eggs?" asked Rooster.

From the expression on Chicken's face, Rooster knew he shouldn't have asked that question. She glared at him and said, "You know very well that I can count my eggs correctly. See for yourself. How many eggs are in my nest?"

"One, two, three," began Rooster. He frowned and stopped counting out loud.

"What's the matter now?" asked Chicken. "Are you afraid to admit you're wrong?"

"No, it's nothing like that at all," replied Rooster. "Something is very wrong here. There are only nine eggs."

"What? Nine Eggs!" cried Chicken. "What is happening? Who would do this to me?"

The next few days were just absolutely terrible for Chicken. Of course, she constantly worried about her remaining eggs. She tried to stay on her nest at all times, but it wasn't possible to always be there. Sometimes she had to leave to get food or take care of her other chicks. No matter why she left, the same thing always happened. One or two eggs disappeared each time.

"Someone is watching me very closely," cried the chicken. "He knows exactly where I am at each moment of the day. I only have three remaining eggs. Three eggs! Can you believe this? I'm down to three eggs in my nest."

"Although I cannot prove anything," said Rooster, "I think it must be Black Snake who is stealing your eggs. We all know that he's patient enough to watch you for a very long time, and everyone knows how he loves to eat eggs."

Just the thought of Black Snake eating her eggs made Chicken shudder. She had heard stories of how he swallowed eggs and then crushed them further down his long slender neck. She knew Rooster was probably correct. But, it really wasn't anything that she wanted to think about very long.

"I must hurry back to my nest," cried Chicken, realizing how long she had talked to Rooster. She rushed back to her eggs, but it was too late. Two more eggs had vanished. "Rooster! Come help me. I only have one egg left."

Rooster came quickly. "You know, it is very likely that Black Snake will steal your last egg tomorrow," he warned. "Unless we can trap him, this will only continue every time you have eggs. And, we have to do something to trap him."

"Yes, it's true," said Chicken, "but what can we do? How can we possibly stop Black Snake?"

"I have a plan," whispered Rooster. "I don't think we will be bothered by him much longer."

The next morning, Chicken continued guarding her last egg as if everything were normal. From a distance, Black Snake couldn't tell that anything had changed. He didn't realize that a deadly trap had been set for him.

Chicken left her nest for only the shortest moment when Black Snake slithered out of hiding.

"One last meal, my little chicken," he whispered. "And, I appreciate it so very much."

In no time at all, he swallowed the final egg. It slid down his throat easily. But, when his muscles squeezed the egg, it did not break. It only became firmly lodged in his throat cutting off his air supply.

Black Snake twisted and turned trying to crush the egg or loosen it so he could breathe. By the time Chicken returned with Rooster, the struggle was over. Black Snake would steal no more eggs.

He was dead.

"I'm sure he died never knowing why that egg didn't crush," crowed Rooster.

"How could he have known," clucked Chicken, "that the egg was hard-boiled?"

SPIDER AND THE HONEY TREE

There was once a young girl from a village far way who had a special talent for finding the very best foods in the bush. Her oranges were just a little sweeter, her plums just a little larger and her bananas had just a little more flavor. Everyone wondered where she located such delicious fruits. But nobody ever asked the girl about her secrets of the bush. That is, nobody asked her after they heard the story about a very greedy Spider and this young girl.

One day Spider asked the girl to help him look for food. He was too lazy to work for himself and was sure he could trick her into sharing her secrets. Unfortunately for him, he didn't know how clever this girl really was.

"Little girl, nobody finds fruits as sweet as yours," said the spider. "Will you please take me with you when you go looking in the bush?"

"I've never done that before," replied the girl.

"It would mean so much if you could do it one time," pleaded Spider.

"Well, I suppose I can do it just once," said the girl. "Do you promise to keep my secrets?"

"You can trust me," promised the lazy spider.

"What do you like to eat?"

"Well, I like plums and bananas, of course, but I especially love honey."

"I think I can help you," replied the girl with a grin.

Spider couldn't believe his luck.

The girl directed Spider along the path into the bush. She took him down trails into areas where people rarely ever go. Spider smiled because he knew he was about to learn her secret places for finding the very best food. After learning this, he would never again have to work hard for a good meal.

"This plum tree," explained the girl, "does not have much fruit, so most people ignore it, but its plums are the sweetest ones in all of the bush."

Now Spider was just as greedy as he was lazy. As soon as the young girl showed him the secret plums, his eyes became wide, and his mouth began to water. Then, Spider shoved the little girl into the bushes. He rushed past her and climbed up into the tree. Then, he ate every single one of the plums. He didn't even leave one plum for the little girl. And, he didn't even say thank you!

ONCE UPON WEST AFRICA

After his feast, Spider rubbed his very full belly and thought, "This is the best day of my life! What a great idea! I can't believe she showed me where her plums are found. I wonder if she will take me to any bananas? She must be very foolish."

Spider looked down at the girl with his biggest smile, and she asked politely, "Do you want any of my special bananas?"

He raced down to her side before the girl could change her mind.

The girl continued down the path showing Spider her secrets of the bush. They walked further down the trail into areas where people rarely ever go. "Over here is a small patch of the very best bananas," said the young girl. Again, as soon as Spider learned the secret, his eyes became wide, and his mouth began to water. Again, he shoved the little girl into the bushes. He rushed past her and climbed the banana plants. He ate every single one of the ripe bananas. Again, he left the young girl with nothing -- not even one banana. And once again, he didn't even say thank you!

His belly was so full, but Spider was not satisfied. He wanted to learn more of the secret places of the bush. He thought to himself, "This girl is really foolish. But, as long as she guides me, I will continue to eat all of her food."

Again, Spider looked at the little girl and smiled. Once again, the young girl looked up at Spider and politely asked, "Would you like to find some honey?"

One more time, Spider rushed to her side and followed the girl down the trail before she had a chance to change her mind.

The young girl guided Spider deeper and deeper into the bush where people rarely ever go. "Over here," she instructed, "is a very special tree. Deep inside a small hole is the most delicious honey in all of the bush."

Now, this girl was not nearly as foolish as Spider thought. She had a plan to teach this greedy spider a lesson. She remembered that Spider loved honey and was not surprised at all when his eyes became wide, and his mouth started to water. She also wasn't surprised when he shoved her into the bushes, ran past her, climbed up the tree and squeezed into the hole. Again, he ate all of the sweet golden honey, sharing nothing with the young girl. He didn't even share one drop. And once again, he didn't even say thank you.

When Spider had eaten his fill, he tried to climb out of the tree, but he couldn't get out of the hole. His stomach had grown too large. He was stuck!

"Help me, young girl," cried the spider. "I cannot get out of the tree!"

"You wouldn't be stuck if you hadn't been so selfish," scolded the girl.

"I'm sorry for what I did! Please call for help," cried Spider.

"I am not as foolish as you think. You aren't sorry for what you did. You are only sorry you are caught in the tree."

"No, you're wrong," lied the spider, but in his heart, he knew she was right. He had enjoyed every minute, every bite of food, as long as he thought he was tricking the young girl. He never expected his idea to turn into such a problem for him. "Please call for help! I am trapped!"

A smile crossed over the little girl's face, and she said she would do as the spider asked. She cried for help as softly as she could. "Help! The foolish spider is caught inside the honey tree. Somebody help this greedy spider!" Of course, nobody heard her whispers for help. And, nobody could hear Spider's cries from deep inside the tree. They were too far into the bush where people rarely ever go.

Finally, the little girl looked up at Spider with a clever grin. "Goodbye, Spider, I am going to get some oranges for my family. If you want to eat some, just follow me there." She waved to him as she left to go down the trail.

THE BEAUTIFUL BRIDE

"Have you heard? Have you heard? Have you heard about the contest?" asked Hippo.

"What contest?" replied Lion.

"Leopard has a contest, and the winner will marry his beautiful daughter," squealed Hippo.

"She is very beautiful," said Goat. "What do I have to do to marry her?"

"This is not a contest for you," snorted Hippo. "This is a contest for big, important animals. Whoever can eat the longest at Leopard's feast will marry the beautiful bride."

"An eating contest? Are you serious?" asked Elephant. "Step aside, boys. I have a wedding that I must prepare for. We all know that nobody can eat more than me."

Maybe nobody could eat more than Elephant, but many wanted to try because Leopard's daughter was so beautiful. Many, many animals wished to marry her.

On the day of the feast, Elephant, Lion, Hippo and several other animals came to the contest. They were big animals, and they were very hungry. It was a good thing that Leopard prepared so much food for the event. Just before the meal and the contest started, Goat said he also wanted to try.

"You must be kidding me! How much can a goat eat?" laughed Elephant.

"He's so small," giggled Lion.

But Leopard said, "My friends, anyone who wants to enter the contest is welcome to try. Sit down, Goat."

When the contest began, most of the guests watched Elephant plow into the food. He ate so much rice and soup that it was hard for Leopard's cooks to even keep up with him! The other animals also ate a lot of food. Well, everyone except for the goat. He slowly took small portions and very carefully chewed his food. He honestly didn't appear to be in any kind of hurry at all.

"Look at Elephant eat!" cried Antelope. "I don't think I can eat that much food in a whole year!"

"And look at poor Goat!" chuckled Monkey. "What is he doing with such a group of eaters?"

"He's certainly not eating like the rest," said Turtle.

Leopard brought more and more food to the table. His wife prepared cassava leaves, jollof rice, palm butter, potato greens, beans gravy and so much more. The animals continued eating. It didn't look like any of them were ever going to stop eating.

It was several hours before Lion pushed his way back from the table. First, he burped. Then, he said, "I give up. I cannot possibly eat another bite. It's all been delicious and I've done my best. But, I cannot eat any more food."

The others continued to eat on and on.

And, on and on.

A few other competitors quit later in the afternoon. But none of them were too surprising. Nobody really expected Antelope or Monkey to win the contest. The big eaters, including Elephant and Hippo, continued feasting. The only real surprise as the competition continued on was Goat. Nobody, especially Elephant and Hippo, thought that Goat had a chance to win. But nobody worried about Goat either. They just continued feasting as they dreamed about their beautiful bride.

A big surprise in the early evening happened the moment that Hippo pushed away from the table. That's right. Hippo gave up before Goat. That meant that only two animals were left. It was down to only Elephant and Goat.

"I cannot believe this," declared Hippo. "How can that little goat eat more than me?"

Elephant didn't have time to say anything. He continued eating and eating. But, if you could read his mind, he was certainly thinking the very same thing that was on everyone's mind. "What was happening with that goat? How was it possible that he was still in this feast?"

Goat said nothing, but just continued slowly chewing his rice.

Elephant smiled to himself. He would soon win the contest. Of that he was certain. However, even he had to admit to himself, he was also feeling a little full. Maybe, a lot more than a little full.

The feast continued late into the night. More palm butter. More potato greens. More jollof rice. It was a feast fit for a king or at least a very worthy groom. And then, much to the surprise of all the animals, at midnight Elephant pushed back from the table. "I can eat no more. Not one more bite! I am just too full. But how can this be? How can a goat eat more than me?"

"He did not eat MORE than you," said Leopard. "This very wise goat ate LONGER than you."

And, then the goat smiled.

"This clever goat had to use his brain as well as his mouth to beat all of you other animals. He ate very slowly and chewed the food carefully. He is very clever to defeat - and out-eat - all of the other contenders. I wanted the one to marry my daughter to be very wise. I am very happy with Goat. Let the wedding begin!"

A DIRTY CONVERSATION

"I can't believe Dog ate all of my food again!" mumbled Cat as she searched for food in the garbage pile. "If I ever get my paws on him, I'll teach that dirty animal a thing or two."

"Who were you calling a 'dirty animal' just now?" barked Dog as he came around the corner of the house.

"You!" hissed Cat. "And, you're also selfish, inconsiderate, rude and impossible!"

"You can't just call me names like that and expect to get away with it," cried Dog in protest.

"I could add to the list if you'd like," replied Cat. "There are so many words that I could choose from. How about smelly?"

"That does it! I will not accept this from you. I'm gonna sue you! You can't slander my good name and not expect me to take action against you," said Dog with a snarl.

"Well, let's go. I have plenty I can say to the judge," Cat replied with a hiss. "Just let me tell her what's on my mind."

The two animals confronted Judge Cow as she quietly ate some grass in the field. Although she never liked a meal interrupted, the judge listened to a few of their complaints. When she realized that there was indeed enough cause for a trial, she called upon Goat, Sheep and Chicken to listen in on the case.

All the animals sat down as Dog explained his problem. "My friends, I am so glad that you are willing to listen to this because I have been so wrongly accused. This cat has treated me poorly," declared Dog. "She has called me 'a dirty animal' and even said that I am 'smelly.' "

Sheep gasped.

"She did it. I promise," said Dog.

"Calling someone 'a dirty animal' is a serious offense in my court," cautioned Judge Cow. "Miss Cat, do you have anything to say in this matter?"

"Do I ever have something to say on the matter! Anything and everything I said was completely justified. This dog has stolen my food for weeks. I am left to search through the garbage to find my meals. I think I have every right to be mad at him AND HE DOES SMELL!"

"If Dog has been eating all of Cat's food, he is certainly selfish, inconsiderate and rude," agreed Cow. "However, that is no reason to call him 'a dirty, smelly animal.' "

"Well, Dog," clucked Chicken, "what do you have to say for yourself? Have you stolen Cat's food?"

The guilty dog was too embarrassed to admit the truth. He only growled.

"I'm going to take that as a 'yes' from you, Mr. Dog," said the judge. "I guess the only thing left to discuss is the charge of calling Dog 'a dirty, smelly animal.' "

"I have a suggestion on how to settle this matter," said Goat. "Since the two animals both live in the same house, let them each take turns going into the humans' bedroom and sitting on the bed. We all know humans worry about cleanliness. They worry way too much about it if you ask me. But, if either animal is truly smelly or dirty, we will certainly hear about it from the humans."

The animals agreed that this plan sounded good. It was decided that since Cat had done the name calling, she should be the first to go in. She promptly left the small group of animals gathered in front of the house and strolled inside.

The woman of the house was resting on the bed when Cat entered the room. The cat jumped up on the bed and curled up on the pillow next to the woman's head. The lady smiled. "My beautiful cat, why are you looking so very thin? Aren't you eating enough? Well, I have a special treat for you today. Come on outside to the front porch, my dear, and I'll give you milk and fish."

Cat couldn't believe her good fortune. Not only was she welcomed on the bed, but she was also treated to a very special meal. And to be given the food in clear view of Dog and the others made the meal taste even more delicious! When the food was finished, Cat strutted back to the small group. "It's your turn, Dog," she spat. "We'll see who is smelly and who isn't."

Dog was every bit as confident as Cat when he entered the house. However, the woman was no longer on the bed. She was cleaning the house. This gave Dog all the room he needed to sprawl out on the bed. When the lady entered the room to sweep, she couldn't believe her eyes. There was Dog, with his head on her pillow, sound asleep.

"You filthy dog!" she screamed. "What are you doing on my bed? Get your head off of my pillow. Who do you think you are? Get out of my house this instant!"

The woman chased the dog out of her bedroom and off of the front porch, hitting him several times along the way with her broom. All of the animals witnessed the incident. Judge Cow declared, "There can be no denying that Cat spoke correctly when she called Dog a 'dirty, smelly animal.' The humans proved that statement is true. I declare court dismissed for the day."

Dog didn't linger around to hear the judgment. He knew what he had to do. When the woman chased him off the porch, he ran past the members of the court and on to the river to quickly take a bath.

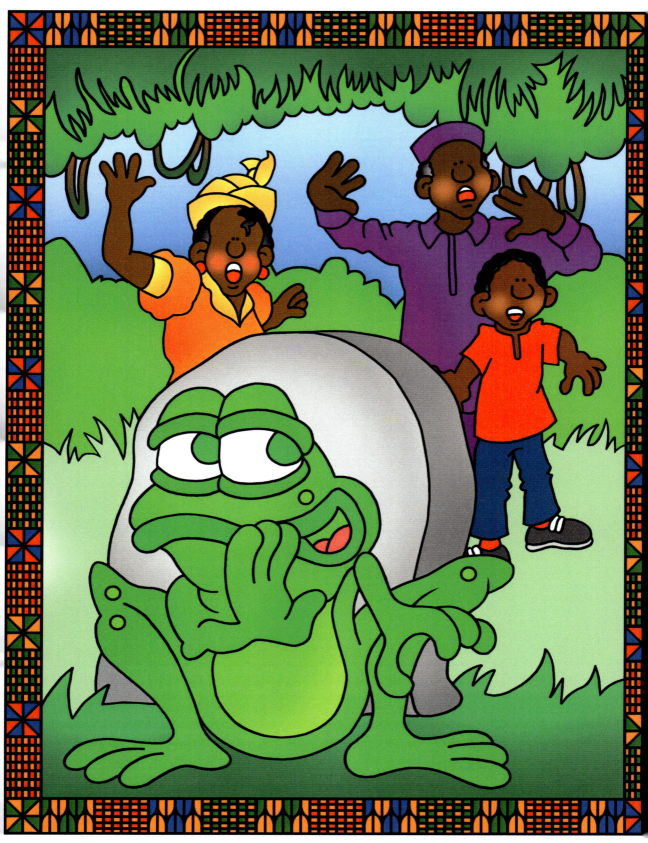

A FRIEND IN TIME OF NEED

In a little village just over the hill lived a young boy named Salgbe. He wasn't a bad boy, but like most boys his age, he sometimes did things that did not please his parents. Frequently, when he should have helped on the farm, Salgbe searched for flies to feed the frog that lived in the field. Instead of gathering firewood, sometimes Salgbe brushed grass away from the big rocks so the lizard could get plenty of sunshine. But the only thing that really vexed his parents was his friendship with Kulba.

Not many people trusted Kulba. Salgbe's parents thought Kulba was a bad influence on their son and tried to keep them separated - but they weren't successful. Kulba was older than Salgbe, and the little boy loved the attention from this young man.

When Kulba married one of the chief's daughters, nobody was happier than Salgbe. However, the happiness was not to last. Three days after the wedding, the chief's daughter mysteriously died. Kulba was accused of using country medicine to kill his bride. The chief sentenced the young groom to death. No one, except for Salgbe, believed Kulba's claim of innocence.

"Tomorrow at noon you will be put to death," declared the chief. "I will kill you over my daughter's grave."

"Kill me if you must," sighed Kulba, "but please let me first say good-bye to my family."

"I cannot permit that," replied the chief with a frown. "You would only run away."

"Where could I go that you and your men could not find me?"

The chief knew this to be true. There was no place Kulba could hide for long. So, the chief permitted Kulba to see his family under one condition. He had to find someone who would stand in for him. If Kulba didn't return by noon the next day, the other person would be killed in his place.

Kulba tried to find someone willing to do this for him, but everyone's reaction was the same. "Are you crazy? If you do not return, I will die. You can just send a letter to your family."

Kulba continued his search. But when Salgbe learned of the problem, he immediately came to his friend's rescue.

"Do you want to die?" cried his mother. "Why are you doing this foolish thing?"

"I will not die, Mother," assured Salgbe. "Kulba is my friend. He will come back for me."

"Tomorrow you will pay the price for your foolishness. Tomorrow you will wish you had listened to your mother."

Kulba was set free to go to his family. The journey was long, and there were many problems. Rains washed away the path and high water destroyed the bridge over the river. On top of that, clouds hid the moon's light, Kulba's lamp went out, and he lost his way in the darkness a few times. It was difficult, but eventually he reached his family.

The following day, the village was alive with anticipation. Would Kulba return? Would Salgbe die in his place? No one knew for sure until everything was answered at noon. Kulba had not returned. So, Salgbe was marched to the grave of the chief's daughter. All was silent except for the sound of one man sharpening a cutlass.

The chief declared, "When I count to ten, you will strike the young boy." Small Salgbe stood bravely, as a man. Kulba was the only friend he would willingly die for. The boy knew there must be a good reason why he did not return. Salgbe would proudly take Kulba's place.

"One, two, three," counted the chief. "Four, five, six."

"Stop!" cried an old man. "I hear something."

Everyone strained to hear if it might be Kulba returning. But there was no sound. There was no trace of Kulba.

"Seven, eight," continued the chief.

"Stop!" cried the old man once again. "There is a voice. I heard something. Listen!"

"Stop, my people," moaned a voice from the grave. "Do not kill this boy."

The people were shocked to hear a voice from the grave. No one had ever heard the dead speak before. Of course, no one realized the voice was actually a frog hiding behind the grave. It was the same frog that Salgbe always fed flies.

"Father, my father," cried the frog, "this is your daughter. I have come back from beyond. Listen to me."

"Is that really you, my daughter?" cried the chief. "What is heaven really like?"

"Heaven is a wonderful place. It is a big swamp, and it always rains. We sit in mud eating flies all day long."

The chief was puzzled. "That doesn't sound very heavenly to me."

But before he could ask another question, he heard another voice. From up in a tree, Salgbe's friend the lizard declared, "This is God."

The chief, elders and villagers all stared up into the sky.

"I am here," bellowed the lizard. "I can see you from heaven."

"What is heaven like?" begged the chief.

"Heaven is a huge rock. We bask in the sun all day eating insects."

"This is too strange," said the chief. "One voice says heaven is wet and the other says heaven is dry. Who can understand the ways of God?"

From the grave, the frog called out, "God?"

"Yes, my daughter, what do you want?" asked the lizard.

"I have a question. If someone dies, even mysteriously, is it proper to put another person to death over their grave?"

"NO! NEVER!" roared the lizard. "If anyone would do such a thing, I would send curses upon him. He would suffer hunger, fever, worms and unspeakable pain."

The chief quickly grabbed the cutlass and hid it behind his back. There would be no killing today if he had anything to say about it.

"I have finished speaking," said the lizard.

The frog also decided it was a good time to be silent. The people stood quietly in awe. Never had they heard from the dead or from God in such a way. It was too amazing. And then, all of a sudden, the silence was broken by a movement in the bushes. Kulba emerged and dragged himself to the gravesite. During the darkness and rains, he had fallen and broken his leg. It had delayed him, but nothing could stop him from returning to rescue his friend.

A GRAVE PROBLEM WITH GREED

"Wife, quickly take my food inside the house," demanded Spider. "I see some strangers coming. If they see my food, they will want to eat some of it."

"Why not share the food?" asked the spider's wife. "We have plenty we could share."

"Did these strangers help me brush the farm?" demanded Spider.

"No, my husband."

"Did they help me plant the seeds?"

"No, again, my husband."

"Did they help me harvest the crops?"

"No. They did not."

"So, why should they expect to eat my food?"

"But, we have plenty of food. It is not good to be so greedy," warned his wife.

Spider was too greedy. Everyone knew that. It was no secret. Not only would he not share the food with strangers, but he also would not share anything with friends. Nearly everyone in town had been insulted at least once when Spider hid food from them. Most of them had experienced it on multiple occasions.

After enough insults, three of the villagers decided it was time to play a trick on Spider. They hid in the bushes near his home and waited until the moment that his wife served Spider a meal. They planned to be so close that Spider would not have time to hide his food. He would have to share with them. There would be no other alternative for him.

Or so they thought . . .

Well, no sooner had Spider taken his first bite of food when the three friends popped out of the bushes. They were right that it was too late for him to hide the food. But they were wrong if they thought the greedy Spider was going to share his meal with anyone, including them. He had another plan. He let out a loud and painful scream. "My wife," cried Spider, "I fear I am dying!"

"Dying! What's the matter, husband?"

The three villagers watched as Spider's wife ran to her husband's side. Nobody believed for one moment that he was actually dying. They had seen too many of his tricks before. They were sure this was just another one. The three sat down to see how this trick would unfold. They knew Spider was stubborn, but just how stubborn was he really?

They were about to find out.

As Spider's wife leaned over her husband, he whispered, "Tell my three friends that I am dead. They will immediately leave to announce the news in the village. In the confusion, they will forget about the food, and we'll be free to finish our meal in peace."

"Seriously? This is your plan?" whispered the wife.

"Yes, do it now," hissed Spider through clenched lips.

Spider's wife did as she was instructed. She turned to her three guests and said, "I am afraid that I must tell you that my husband has died. Can you please go tell the others in the village about this?"

But the plan didn't go as Spider had expected. The three villagers quickly replied, "We are sorry for his death. He was such a dear friend. Before we go to the village to share this sad news, we feel that we should help you here. If you get a shovel, we will bury Spider for you. It is the least we can do for our friend."

Mrs. Spider did not really know what she should do under the circumstances. But her husband hissed, "Go get the shovel."

So, that's exactly what she did.

After giving the three men the shovel, Spider's wife directed the men to a spot behind the house. As they dug the hole in the ground, she rushed back to her husband's side.

"Husband," she cried, "stop this foolishness! This is absolutely crazy. How can you possibly be so greedy? Food is not worth dying for. Share some with our guests."

"I would rather die," replied the stubborn spider, "than let these men eat one bite of my rice."

"What's the matter with you? It's just rice!"

In tears, Spider's wife went back to check on the guests. They were nearly finished with the hole. She rushed back to her husband one more time to change his mind. "It is always better to live. Please share your food," she begged.

Spider made no reply. He had made up his mind and nothing was going to change it. He would not share with these men even if it killed him. There was no turning back.

When the hole was completed, the three men returned for Spider's body.

"Just give me another minute alone with him," pleaded Spider's wife. She could not hold back her tears. "Spider," she whispered, "change your mind before it is too late!"

But Spider made no reply.

He was too stubborn and entirely too greedy to share his rice harvest. There was absolutely nothing else his wife could do or say. No amount of begging would change his mind. Eventually, Spider's sobbing wife stepped aside and allowed the three men to bury her husband in his freshly dug grave.

A LESSON IN MANNERS

There was once a boy who loved to boast. He boasted about everything and he did this all the time. He claimed that he could run faster than everyone else. He bragged that he, of course, wore the nicest clothes. But, his very favorite topic, which everyone heard over and over, was his education. Too many times to count, he declared loud and long, "I attend the city school, as you might know, while everyone else I know stays home and goes to the little school in the village."

"Yes, we know all about it," everyone muttered. Always.

Still, the boy had to continue, "I think I have a fine education and I just wanted to make sure that everyone knows it."

"We have been told . . . repeatedly," everyone also muttered.

It's not like the boy wasn't raised well. His parents honestly tried to teach him about manners and respect. The boy just thought he knew more than both his father and his mother.

"Boasting is not good," warned his mother. "It's not good at all. You misuse your knowledge when you use it to . . ."

". . . make others feel small," interrupted the boy. He'd heard this line enough to certainly finish the sentence. The lesson just never sank into his brain.

"It sounds to me like you are jealous of all my wisdom," scoffed the boy. He left the house, headed in the direction of the market. Sometimes, he liked to see who he could impress with all the facts he knew. Nobody was ever as impressed as he was with himself.

The first person the boy encountered was a man selling country cloth shirts at the market. The boy asked, "Do you know how to do anything other than make silly old cloth?"

"This cloth is part of our culture," replied the man. "I learned how to make it from my father."

"Well, I go to school in the city for my learning, so I am really educated. I know all kinds of things. Do you know the meaning of 'environment'? It's one of the new words I learned at my school . . . my school in the city."

"No, son, I have never heard of that word before," replied the old man. "However, I've lived a long life and I know a great many things you'll never learn in your books."

"Then, they must not be important," chuckled the boy.

ONCE UPON WEST AFRICA

The old man had no plans to teach the boy about respect and manners, not yet anyway. But he knew he had his fill concerning the child's education.

"Can you spell the word 'traditional'? I think that is an easy word."

"I know my country cloth is traditional," replied the old man. "But, no, I cannot spell the word."

"It must be terrible not to know these things," sighed the boy.

"I know there are much more important things in life," said the old man, but the boy had no clue what he meant.

"Don't you wish you were educated like me? Isn't it strange that I am so young and know so much that I've learned at my school . . . in the city . . . and you are so old and know so little? Old man, where were you educated?"

"It was not in the city at your school."

"Isn't that such a shame?"

Now, the old man was a patient person, but he'd had about all of the boy's education he could stand. He knew exactly what to do with this boaster and how to teach him a lesson that he'd never forget. The old man looked at the boy and said, "Son, I'd like to show you what I do know. I didn't learn it from books, but it may be something you will consider extremely important."

Now the boy was really interested. He wondered, "What could this old man possibly know that I would ever consider important? He isn't educated like me." Certainly, the old man had figured out how to capture his attention. The boy had to follow him and find out what was so important.

The two walked through the village and down to the river's edge. The old man directed the boy into a dugout canoe. Each took an oar, and together they set out for the other side of the river.

The man looked at the boy and said, "You will soon see what I have learned."

"I hope it is worth the effort. Are you sure I will consider this important?" asked the boy.

"I am quite certain," the old man assured him.

"Really?"

That was the last question and the last straw for the old man. They were in the deepest part of the river, where the current was the swiftest. Without warning, the old man tipped the canoe on purpose. They both fell into the current.

The old man swam quickly to the shore, leaving the boy struggling in the water. From the edge of the river, he called out to the boy, "Do you know the word 'manners'? Can you spell the word 'polite'? I know these words, and I never learned them in your books! I learned them from my parents. Have you learned anything from your father? Do you listen to your mother?"

The proud boy realized there are also important things to learn that are not in books. Certainly, the old man knew something the boy now considered very important. The old man could swim! Unfortunately for the boy, he learned the lesson too late.

A SCRAMBLED FRIENDSHIP

Little Chicken and Egg had been close friends ever since anyone could remember. If Little Chicken went shopping at the market, Egg was at her side. If Egg had trouble with his schoolwork, Little Chicken helped him figure it out. They lived, worked and played together all the time. Their Auntie Chicken put them to bed every night. She loved them and took good care of them. But, their friendship was put to the test when Auntie Chicken had to leave for one week.

"Now listen to me, my little ones," said Auntie Chicken. "I will not be gone so long. I need you to be all grown up and take care of yourselves. Can you do that for me?"

"Of course, we can!" both of them agreed.

"That's what I thought you would say. Thank you so much," replied Auntie Chicken.

The two friends had the best of intentions, and their auntie put all her trust in them. However, sometimes, you need more than the best of intentions. This was one of those times.

"Both of you have to help take care of yourselves while I am gone," explained their auntie. "And, in order to do that, it means that you have to share the work equally."

"We can do that," they both promised.

So, they had a plan when their auntie left. Yes, they had a plan. Yes, they were supposed to follow it. At least, that was the way things were supposed to work out.

On the first day of the week, Little Chicken washed clothes and prepared their evening meal. "Look, Egg, I made cassava leaves for you," she clucked, "because I know it is your favorite."

"Thank you so much," replied Egg. "You know me so well, and it is so appreciated."

Little Chicken smiled. She appreciated the kind words, but she also suspected it meant she would have beans gravy the following day. It was, after all, her favorite meal. And, fair is fair. If she could make cassava leaves, the least Egg could do the next day was to make her favorite dish.

After the meal, Egg cleared the table, washed the dishes and put everything away. All went very well that first day. In fact, it could not have been any better.

But then, there was the second day.

The jobs were traded on the second day. It was Egg's turn to wash clothes and prepare the meal. Little Chicken was to clean and dry the dishes before putting them away. That was the plan. And, sometimes, plans don't always go the way they are supposed to go.

Little Chicken suspected that something was not right as soon as she came home for the evening meal. "Hmm . . . I don't smell anything delicious coming from the kitchen," she said. "I don't even smell anything bad coming from the kitchen. There is no smell coming out of the kitchen, and there really should be the smell of beans gravy."

Egg did not say anything.

"What is there to eat?" demanded Little Chicken.

Egg still did not say anything.

"I give up. I can't smell anything. What did you prepare?"

Egg wouldn't even look Little Chicken in the eye.

Little Chicken scratched around the kitchen looking for any kind of meal. But, there was nothing to be found. No food was prepared. Nothing. Absolutely nothing!

"What have you done all day? Where is my food?" demanded Little Chicken. "Today was your turn to cook the food!"

Finally, without looking at his friend, Egg declared, "I don't like to cook, so I didn't prepare anything."

"What? No food? Did you wash the clothes?" asked Little Chicken.

Again, he couldn't look his friend in the eye. Finally, Egg said, "No, I don't like to wash clothes either."

Little Chicken was really vexed with Egg.

She fully knew how hard she had worked on the first day. And, she prepared cassava leaves! Egg should have worked equally hard the second day. It just wasn't right.

"You are one rotten egg!" shouted Little Chicken.

The words slipped out of her mouth before she really thought about their impact. And, isn't that how it often happens? It really was the worst thing she could have called Egg.

He turned around, looked his friend in the eye, and said, "You're just street meat waiting to be eaten." Again, not something you should really say to your friend. At least, if your friend is a chicken.

And, that's how the fight started.

It was a terrible fight that should never have happened between two friends. But, Little Chicken was frustrated, angry and so very hungry that she couldn't think clearly. And, of course, Egg really had been lazy and treated his friend unfairly. So, they fought. In a moment of absolute frustration, the hungry chicken just opened her mouth and swallowed the egg. Yes, that's right. You read it correctly. She opened up her mouth and swallowed him whole! And once that happened, there was no going back. Some things you just can't undo.

That was how it all began so long ago with chickens laying eggs. When chickens see the unbroken circle that an egg forms, they are reminded of a good friendship that should never have been broken. Kind words, at all times, can keep an egg from cracking and a friendship from scrambling.

CAT DREAMS WHILE RAT SCHEMES

All the animals in the bush knew that Cat and Rat were very good friends. On cold nights, Rat used to sleep in Cat's arms to keep warm. On hot days, Rat used to bring cool milk to refresh Cat. They lived in the same house, ate the same food and drank palm wine together. It was difficult to ever see Cat without Rat by his side.

One day Rat had an idea. "My good friend, Cat," he said, "I am happy that we are such good friends. We get along so well that I think we should also make a cassava farm together. The work would not seem so hard if the two of us worked side by side."

"I think that's an excellent idea, my friend," replied Cat. "If we make a cassava farm, then we could make plenty of dumboy, fufu and cassava leaves. And you know, I believe you can never have too many cassava leaves."

"I know that," continued Rat with a smile. "And, I think that if two of us worked together, we could make a very big farm and also sell the cassava. We would have plenty to eat as well as plenty of money to spend."

"Yes," agreed Cat, "and with two of us our efforts will be cut in half."

"And, the work will be twice as fun," added Rat.

It was agreed, and the two friends made an unusually large cassava farm. Together, they brushed the field. Together, they burned the bush. Together, they scratched the ground and planted the cassava sticks. Together, they weeded the farm. Finally, they sat back together as the months passed to plan how they would spend all of their money they were going to make.

"I dream of buying cement to plaster the house," said Cat.

"You'll probably need a few bags to do it."

"What do you want to buy with your share of the money, Rat?"

"Well, I can tell you I'm not going to buy any cement. I plan to go to the city where I will buy only the finest clothes. Then, I want to eat at only the best restaurants and be seen with all of the right people. Yes, I want a fine trip to the big city."

"That's an excellent dream. It would be a fine thing to do," agreed Cat, "but it would also be so expensive. There is nothing cheap about a trip to the city."

Rat was well aware of that.

And, the little rat also had a plan. While Cat was a dreamer, Rat was a schemer. If that's a new word for you, a schemer is someone who makes secret and underhanded plans. Yes, Rat was a schemer.

He knew that it would be very expensive to go to the city. But, Rat didn't want to just go to the city. He wanted to move there. And, that would take a lot of money, more money than Rat rightfully had. However, he had a plan that he had been considering for months. His plan was both secret and so very underhanded.

One day when the cassava was nearly ready to harvest, Rat went to visit Leopard.

"Hello, my dear friend," said Rat. "How are you today?"

"I'm doing well," replied Leopard. "You are a ways from home. What brings you here today?"

"Well, I have a proposition. It's a bargain that I don't think you can possibly pass on."

"Okay," replied Leopard. "You have my attention. What are you talking about?"

"I have a cassava farm that I would like to sell to you. I've done all the brushing, planting and caring for the farm. The only thing left to do is harvest."

"Now, is this the same farm that you've been making with Cat?"

"Of course," replied Rat. "He's aware of all of this. He wants to sell the farm as much as I do."

"A farm like that would be worth a lot of money. May I ask what you want to do with that much cash?"

"I want to go to the city," replied the rat.

"And, will Cat go with you?"

"No, I will be going alone."

"And your friend is fine with this? It's really okay with him to sell the farm after all this work?"

"Absolutely," lied the little rat.

"Well, in that case, I will gladly buy the farm," said Leopard. He paid the large sum of money Rat was asking for it.

It will probably come as no surprise that Rat never told any of this to Cat. Of course, he never shared any of the money with him either. He slipped out of the village in the dark of night and headed to the big city with all the cash.

Poor Cat had no idea what had happened to his friend. He searched the village for him. Nobody had seen Rat for days. He looked all over the bush with no luck. Finally, he checked at the cassava farm. To his surprise, there was Leopard harvesting the cassava. "Rogue!" cried Cat. "What are you doing in my cassava farm?"

"It's MY cassava farm," answered Leopard. "Didn't you know I bought it from Rat before he left for the city?"

"The city? What are you talking about?"

"I think I need to tell you about your friend," said the leopard.

It was at that moment when Cat realized his best friend was also his secret enemy. Of course, their friendship was ruined. There was no way that was ever going to be repaired. Rat proved just how little he cared about it. And as for Cat, he was certain that he would have his revenge if he ever found that scheming rat.

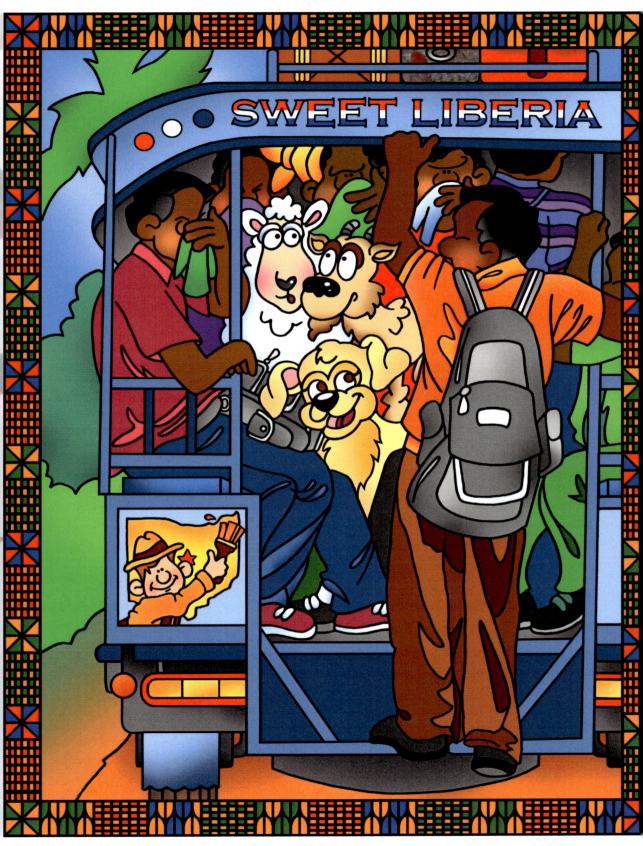

FREE RIDE?

"How much does it cost to reach town?" asked Dog.

"It is a $2.50 distance," replied the driver. "If you are coming, you must get in the truck now. We're ready to go."

The back of the old truck had three long wooden benches for passengers. It was already very crowded when Dog squeezed in between Goat and Sheep. Fortunately, the driver was right, and it wasn't long before the truck took off down the long dirt road. Most of those in the back of the truck tried to hide their faces because the red dust along the roadside was so very thick.

"I'll be glad when we have a little bit of rain to settle this dust," cried Goat.

"Me too!" coughed Sheep.

The trip to town was uneventful. There were a few police checkpoints and a stop to buy gasoline. Just before reaching the town, the driver stopped his truck to collect his money. Like most passengers, Sheep paid her $2.50 to the driver. Dog only had $5.00 and expected to get his change as soon as the driver had collected money from everyone else. However, there was a problem that neither Dog nor the driver realized. Goat had no money to pay for his ride. And, he had no intention of paying. Since Dog was sitting next to Goat, the driver assumed Dog had paid for the two of them. He didn't plan on giving Dog any change.

The moment the truck pulled into the parking station, Goat jumped out and ran away. Dog, on the other hand, waited for most of the passengers to leave and then helped Sheep down from the truck. Just as Dog turned around to get his change from the driver, the truck pulled away.

"Wait!" cried Dog. "What about my change? You owe me $2.50!"

The dog ran after the driver but was unable to catch him. Sheep just stood where she was watching everything. She had paid for her ride. The problem was really between Dog and Goat.

Although this story took place a long time ago, there are constant reminders of this even today. Watch carefully the next time you ride in a truck. Sheep will just stand in the road. After all, she paid her fare, so the truck does not bother her. Goat, afraid that the driver might be the one he never paid, will run into the bushes and hide. Finally, you can be sure Dog will run after the truck barking. If you could understand his words, you'd hear him cry, "Where's my change? Where's my change?"

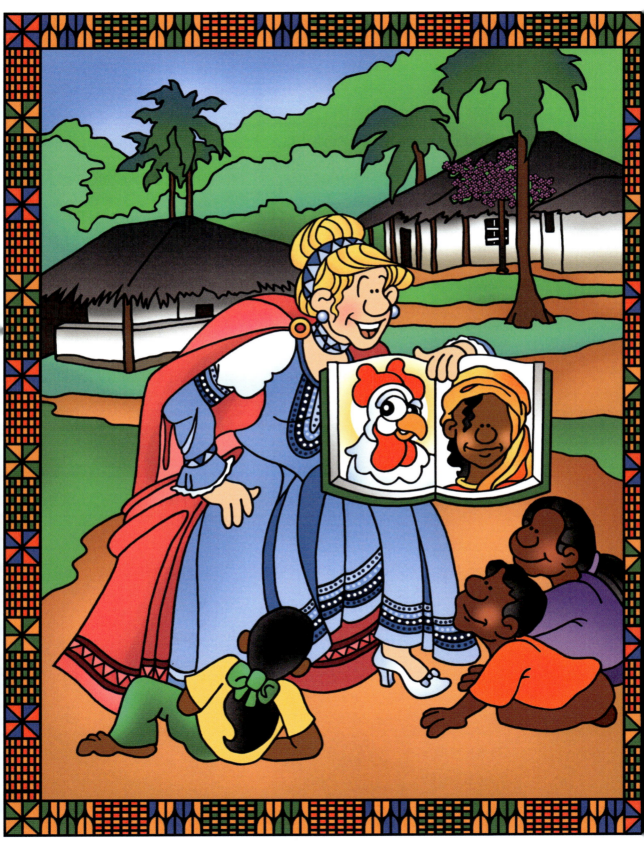

MUSU, BENDU AND CINDERELLA

A long time ago, there once lived a beautiful girl who lived with her evil step-mother and wicked step-sisters. That was Cinderella, but this story out of Africa has a familiar theme. However, did you ever wonder what happened to the evil step-sisters? In this Liberian tale, you're about to find out just what happened to those people who were so unfair to Cinderella . . . er, Musu.

When Musu's mother died, another one of the chief's wives said she would take care of her. It appeared to be a good arrangement because the woman already had a daughter, Bendu, about the same age as Musu. As it turned out, however, it was a sad situation for Musu. The mother loved Bendu. In her eyes, she could do nothing wrong, and Musu could do little right.

"Musu, isn't the food ready yet? You are such a lazy child!" scolded the mother. "Why can't you be more like Bendu?"

"I'm sorry, Mother," apologized Musu. "I will work harder."

Neither Bendu nor her mother did any work around the home. It was Musu's responsibility to make the rice farm, grow vegetables, hunt for meat, harvest rice, prepare food and wash clothes. Musu even had to make her own soap and sew her own clothes. There was no caring, appreciation or love for Musu in this house.

As if things couldn't get worse, one day while Musu was pounding rice, a white chicken flew into the mortar and Musu accidentally killed it. It all happened so suddenly!

"How could you be so careless?" screamed the mother. "Don't you realize that genies live in white chickens? We are never to harm them. They will soon come for you because you killed this chicken. See if you can finish all of your work before they arrive."

It wasn't long before the yard was filled with hundreds of white chickens. The chickens arrived with a hammock and were prepared to carry Musu away. No amount of begging would change their minds.

"Oh, please don't carry me away," begged Musu. "It was an accident. I didn't mean to kill your white chicken. I'll do anything I can to make up for this. The chickens would not listen to her pleas, and eventually, Musu climbed into the hammock to be carried off to the genies' hill.

The chief genie greeted her warmly. "Do not be afraid, Musu. We know you. We knew your mother. We know how you have suffered since your mother died. We will take care of you."

Musu was directed to a small room where she could rest. The floor had been recently swept, and there was a small mat for her in the corner. The genies provided Musu with some food and said they would return when she had rested. After eating, Musu curled up on her mat to take a nap.

She hadn't slept long when she heard a noise at the door.

"Who is it?" asked Musu.

"It is Dog," replied the voice. "Please let me enter."

Musu opened the door to see a very wretched dog. He obviously hadn't eaten anything in days. She couldn't help but wrap her arms around him.

"I know you are a stranger here," continued the dog, "and I know the genies always feed their guests. Do you have a bone I could eat?"

"A bone? Nonsense!" cried Musu. "You need good food. Here, have the rest of my rice and soup. I had plenty. Please finish it."

The dog ate the food and then found a warm corner in the room where he could sleep.

Not long afterward, there was another knock at the door. This time it was an old woman.

"Please come in and sit down," offered Musu.

"Thank you, my dear. I am so tired, and my leg hurts so badly."

Musu looked down at the old woman's leg. There was a bad sore that desperately needed cleaning. After washing the sore, Musu used part of her scarf to bandage the leg. She led the old woman to her mat and urged her to get some rest.

No sooner had Musu settled the old woman down on the mat than there was another knock at her door. "Who could that be?" she wondered. "This certainly is a busy place!"

This time an old man with a bag entered her room.

"My daughter, have you been to school? Can you count?" asked the old man.

"Yes, I can do that," replied Musu.

"Please, will you count the money in this bag for me?" pleaded the old man. "I am a tailor and have saved a long time to buy a sewing machine."

"I will certainly help you," replied Musu. She emptied a bag of coins on to the floor. The old man excused himself while Musu counted the coins.

He was very pleased when he returned because he already knew the exact amount. Musu had been truthful when she handed him his money. "You have been very good to the three of us," declared the old man.

"Tomorrow you will be brought before the genie chief and asked to select one of ten boxes. One has great wealth, but the others contain terrible troubles. If you select the wrong box, you will get malaria, blindness, snakes, worms or even death."

"What should I do?" wailed Musu.

"We will help you," replied the old woman with a comforting smile. "Select the box that the dog rests beside. It will be the same box that I will sit upon."

"The tailor will comment that it is an ugly box," barked the dog. "That is the box you should choose."

Musu listened carefully to their instructions. In the morning she was brought before the chief genie and shown ten boxes. Some were big and colorful while others were small and plain. Some were old, and others were new. Some were locked while others were not.

The old woman sat on an iron box. The dog rested at her feet. The tailor asked the woman why she sat on such an ugly box. Musu recognized all of the clues and followed their instructions. She selected the black iron box.

The genies were very pleased.

When the box was opened, Musu discovered all kinds of riches. She took her treasures back to her village and built her own home. She no longer had to suffer with Bendu and her mother. Eventually, she married and had many children. Their home was filled with laughter and love.

This is as close as an African folk tale gets to "and they all lived happily ever after." But, they all didn't. Now in Cinderella, we never do learn if the evil step-mother and step-sisters get what they deserved. However, there is more to this story. In fact, it is only half-finished.

Meanwhile, back at Bendu's house, things only became worse after Musu left. Bendu only knew how to dress nicely. She had never worked and certainly didn't know how to make a farm or cook. Her mother complained continually. Neither of them realized all the work Musu had done until she was gone. The two of them together were not able to do as much work as Musu had managed alone.

"If only you, instead of Musu, had killed that white chicken," complained the mother. "We could be rich!"

Suddenly, an idea formed in the mother's head. Bendu could kill a white chicken just as Musu had done! Then, Bendu would also get some treasures. It was so obvious, so simple! Why had she not thought of it earlier?

Killing a white chicken was not as easy as Bendu expected. She chased one in the yard with her knife. She cornered another in her house with a basket. They always escaped. Finally, to her delight, she managed to kill one when she pounded rice in the mortar.

Bendu and her mother were so excited. They already had her clothes packed when the chickens came with their hammock for Bendu. That didn't surprise the chickens as much as Bendu's words.

"I'm not getting in that dirty hammock," muttered Bendu. "I'll walk with you. Here, you can carry my bags."

As Bendu walked down the path with the chickens, her mother called out, "Don't forget to tell the chief genie you want a box. Maybe even three or four of them!"

Bendu thought it was a very long walk to the hill where the chief genie lived. Before the chief had a chance to welcome Bendu officially, she blurted out, "Where's my treasure? That's why I'm here."

The chief genie directed her to her room. It was the same room where Musu had stayed. Although the chickens prepared the room, Bendu was not pleased. "Who cleaned this? Has it ever been swept? I can't stay in a room like this!"

The chickens were very embarrassed.

The genie chief left as Bendu's meal was delivered. "What kind of soup is this?" she cried. "It's simply disgusting! I can't eat this. Just give me my treasures and let me go home."

As the chickens removed the soup to try again, Bendu noticed the mat on the floor. "Where's my bed? I can't sleep on that!"

The chickens had enough. They left Bendu alone in her room.

Bendu sat down on the mat and pouted. Things were not going as planned.

A little while later, there was a knock at the door. Bendu was dismayed to see it was just a miserable dog.

"What do you want?" she demanded.

"Please, I'm very hungry," said the dog. "Could you share some food?"

"Get away from here, you miserable dog. They already took my soup. I only have rice, and I'm not about to share with you," screamed Bendu as she slammed the door.

Shortly afterward there was another knock at the door. Bendu got up to chase the dog away again, but to her surprise, there was a woman at the door.

"What do you want? Can't you see I want to be alone?"

"I'm sorry, my child," apologized the old woman. "My leg is hurting me. Can you help me?"

"Take your smelly leg away from here! It's making me sick. I'm not a nurse. I'm only here to get my fortune," snarled Bendu.

As the old woman left, the tailor approached with his bag of money.

"Money!" squealed Bendu with delight. She snatched it from the man's hands and shut the door in his face. When she sat down to count it, she was very upset with the small number of coins in the pile.

There was no waiting until the next morning for Bendu. She immediately stormed out of the room and boldly marched up to the chief genie. "What do you mean only giving me such a small amount of coins when you gave Musu so many treasures?"

"Musu received her gift when she selected a box," explained the genie chief. "There are ten boxes here before you. Select one for yourself. Many have sickness and troubles, but one has more treasure than you can imagine."

The dog ran away from the boxes. The old woman stood by watching. The tailor said nothing as Bendu selected the biggest box with brightly colored ribbons. She proudly carried it home to her mother. The mother and daughter opened the box together. To their horror, it was full of terrible diseases. The two became very sick and died before the day was over.

It is safe to say that they did not live happily ever after.

HOW NOT TO MAKE A FARM

As Spider carried his cutlass into the bush, he met Monkey. It was time to make a farm, and both of the animals were searching for a good spot in the bush. Monkey had just come from the blacksmith's shop, and so his cutlass was very sharp.

"I enjoy brushing and cutting down the trees," said Monkey. "I can brush all day and not get tired."

"Not me," replied Spider. "I do not like to brush, not one little bit. But I enjoy making a fence around the farm. I don't use wood though. I use the rope from my web. It's very strong, you know."

"You are so very fortunate, Spider. Making the fence is the part I do not enjoy."

"Maybe we should make a big farm together?" suggested Spider. "You can brush the farm while I make the fence. We can make a farm big enough to feed both of our families."

"That's an excellent idea. Let's begin tomorrow."

"And if our wives bring us food each day," offered Spider, "we'll get the work completed even faster."

"That's another good idea, Spider. Since it was your idea, your wife should bring the food on the first day."

Now, Spider didn't like that idea one little bit. He didn't want his wife to be the first one to prepare the food. However, he didn't see any way to refuse. The following day, the work on the farm began. Monkey slashed all day with his cutlass while Spider carefully spun his web. Monkey seriously wanted to rest some, but since Spider wasn't stopping, he couldn't take a break. Truth be told, Spider also was tired but was too embarrassed to stop while Monkey worked. Each animal was vexed with the other for working so hard.

Finally, when Spider's wife came with a bowl of palm butter and a large pot of rice, Spider decided to play a trick on Monkey. Both Spider and Monkey were very pleased as they sat down to eat. Spider watched as Monkey began to reach for a handful of rice.

"Wait!" cried Spider. "Did you wash your hands before eating?"

Monkey was very embarrassed. Very quickly, he raced to the stream to wash his hands. When he returned, Spider had already started eating the palm butter.

"Do you really think your hands are clean?" asked the spider. "Look! They are still dirty. Are you trying to spoil my food by eating with dirty hands? Go wash your hands again."

Once again, Monkey went to the stream. This time he washed all the way to his elbows. When he finished, he rushed back to Spider. By this time he was very hungry. All the while, Spider continued eating.

Spider wiped some palm oil from his mouth and asked, "Are you sure your hands are clean? Let me see them."

When Monkey showed him his hands, Spider shook his head. "They are still dirty! Do you want me to get sick? How can I make our fence if I am sick?"

"But my hands are not dirty at all!" cried the hungry monkey. "They are completely clean. Why do you treat me like this? How could my hands make you sick?"

"Don't you know that dirty hands can spread germs that cause sickness? Go wash your hands one more time," demanded Spider as he put some more rice in his mouth.

Monkey quickly washed his hands again. When he returned, Spider grinned broadly. "You don't have to worry about getting me sick with your dirty hands. I have finished the rice. Thank you for trying to get your hands clean."

"You're welcome," mumbled the monkey.

The next day, work continued on the farm, but the two friends didn't speak much to each other. When Spider stopped his spinning, Monkey said he was lazy. When Monkey paused from his brushing, Spider accused him of being a small boy. They were both tired and hungry by the time Monkey's wife brought her special beans gravy.

"What is this soup?" asked Spider.

"You don't know what it is?" replied Monkey as he grabbed the bowl. "I cannot let you eat something that you do not recognize. Perhaps it is your taboo. Take one of these flat round things from the soup and show it to your wife. She will know what it is and if you may eat it."

Spider thanked Monkey for his thoughtfulness and quickly ran off to his wife. He pleaded, "What is this flat round thing? I know it is not an onion or an eggplant. Is it cassava? Is it our taboo?"

"It is only a bean, my husband," assured Spider's wife. "We never eat them because I do not like them. They are not, however, our taboo."

"Thank you," said Spider.

"Bean, bean, bean," he repeated on the way back to the farm. Spider was so busy repeating the name that he didn't pay attention to where he walked. He tripped on a stone, cut his toe and dropped the bean. When he arrived back at the farm, his mind was on the accident.

"Well," asked the monkey, "do you know what kind of soup this is? Can you eat it?"

"Yes, it's bitter ball soup," said the spider with a wide grin.

"I know it is not bitter ball soup," replied the monkey. "Go back quickly and again ask your wife about the soup. Hurry! I don't want your part of the soup to get cold."

Again, Spider rushed off to his wife. "What was the name of that soup?"

When she repeated that it was beans gravy, Spider headed back into the bush repeating, "Bean, bean, bean, bean . . ." Again, he wasn't paying attention. Again, he had another accident. He fell into the river this time. When Spider finally reached back to the farm, he could not remember the name of the soup.

Monkey just laughed. "It's not important anymore. The food was getting cold, so I finished it. It doesn't matter if it was your taboo. It was very good and, just in case you were wondering, I remembered to wash my hands."

MAN FORGIVES AN ENEMY AND FINDS A FRIEND

"We all agree that it is not good to have Man living in our village," said Leopard.

"That's true, of course," bleated Goat, "but do you have any idea what we can do about it?"

"I don't think there is anything we can do," growled Dog. "I think he's here to stay."

"Oh, my friends," replied Leopard with a smile, "there is always a solution to every problem. You just need to set your mind to it. I have done that, and I think I have the perfect idea."

Leopard's plan was very simple.

Goat, Dog and Leopard would have Man join them on a farm. Each day a different member of the farm was to bring the food with fresh meat for all of the farmers. Anyone not bringing meat would be killed. Since the three animals were good hunters, this rule was no problem for them. However, Man had never hunted animals in the bush before. He would surely fail and then be killed. The animals' problem would be solved.

"I like that plan," said Goat.

"But do you think we can get Man to agree to it?" asked the dog.

"Trust me," promised Leopard. "He is too proud to say no to this. Man will agree to our plan."

Leopard was right. Man agreed to help make the farm, but he was very concerned about the special rule. He had never hunted before, so he was nervous.

The first day they worked on the farm, Leopard brought the meat. "It was easy for me to catch several deer," he boasted. Everyone knew he was a proud hunter. The meal was proof of his talents.

On the second day, Goat brought a few deer. "Since I look so much like the deer, it was easy for me to sneak up on them," laughed the goat. "They never saw me coming."

Dog, also an excellent hunter, had no trouble providing meat on the third day. "I might not look like a monkey," he barked, "but it was no problem for me to catch a few for this meal."

So, the pressure was on. Everyone waited to see what would happen with Man on the fourth day. And, to be honest, Man was very worried as well. He didn't know how to catch any meat. But, he had been thinking about what to do.

"I need some help," thought Man. "Maybe the native doctor can give me some country medicine to catch some meat? I've learned it never hurts to ask. And, I certainly need help."

So, that's just what the man did. He went to the native doctor. And, very fortunately for him, the native doctor was able to help with the problem.

"Take this animal horn filled with my special powder," instructed the native doctor. "When you see an animal, throw some powder in the air and command the animal to die. It's very strong medicine. It'll do just what you ask."

"That's really all I need to do?" asked the man.

"As I told you, it's very strong medicine," replied the native doctor.

Man thanked him and went into the bush to hunt. Even though he had no experience as a hunter, it didn't take him long to find three deer. And, he knew what to do. He threw some powder into the air and commanded, "You three deer, you must die."

Instantly, the three animals fell over dead.

"That was simple," thought the man. "This should be enough meat for us. I'll return to the village now."

Nobody expected Man to successfully catch anything. Everyone was excited to see just how the hunting trip would turn out. As for Leopard, he could hardly wait to kill Man just as soon as he admitted his failure. So, it must be said that it completely amazed all of the villagers when Man stepped out of the bushes with three deer.

"How did you get that meat?" demanded Dog. "It really isn't possible that you can catch three deer."

"You can't hunt! What did you do?" asked Goat. "Seriously, how did this happen?"

"Just forget about it, my friends," cautioned Man. "If I show you what I did, you will die."

"Nobody believes that threat and nobody believes you," snarled Leopard. "Now, tell us right away how this happened."

"Immediately!" snorted the goat.

"It's time to tell us the truth," barked Dog.

"Well, if you insist. Remember, I did warn you about this." The man pulled the horn out of his pocket and threw some powder in the air. "Leopard, I command you to die."

The leopard instantly fell over.

Dead.

Then, the man looked at Goat and threw some more powder in the air. "I command you to die, Goat."

The goat instantly fell over.

Also, dead.

Finally, the man looked at Dog as he threw some more powder into the air. "Dog, I command you to ... "

"WAIT!!" cried Dog. "Do not finish that sentence. Do not kill me. Please, I'm begging you to forgive me. I am sorry I ever troubled you. From now on, if you have mercy, I promise that I will follow after you and take care of all your needs. I will protect you and be your friend."

Man put away his powder without finishing that sentence. "I accept your offer, Dog," he declared. And from that day on, Man and Dog have always remained the best of friends.

MANJO AND THE CROCODILE

Manjo was known throughout the village as the best hunter. He had a secret that made him so good. He always looked in four places every time he went hunting. He searched in the river, on the ground, up the trees and across the sky. When he searched in these four places, he always found something to shoot.

One day Manjo searched the river, but there were no fish. There were no birds in the sky and no animals on the ground. There was, however, to his great surprise, a crocodile up in a tree.

"Crocodiles can't climb trees. How did you get up there?" demanded Manjo.

"How do you know we can't climb trees?" replied the crocodile.

"Everyone knows that."

"Well, sometimes everyone is wrong. Even my book here says crocodiles can't climb trees."

"What kind of book is that?" asked Manjo.

"It's called <u>How Crocodiles Are Supposed to Act</u>. All of us must study it when we go to crocodile school."

"Crocodile school?"

"Of course, we meet at the bottom of the river. Would you like to look at my book?"

How could he say no? Manjo was amazed with the book. There were chapters on "How to Swim," "How to Catch Fish," "How to Walk on Four Legs," "How to Stay Underwater" and even "How to Catch People." Manjo didn't read any of that final chapter and especially didn't want to look at the pictures.

"My favorite chapter is 'Things That are Too Hard for Crocodiles to Do.' I already know how to do things like fishing and swimming," said the crocodile, "so I like to try more difficult tasks. I enjoy being the first crocodile to do something. I've already learned to walk on two legs. I use my tail to balance me. Now, I'm the first crocodile to climb a tree."

The crocodile leaned back and smiled. He was obviously very proud of himself. Suddenly, he slipped and nearly fell out of the tree.

Manjo struggled not to laugh.

"There is one problem I must admit," confessed the crocodile. "I still haven't learned how to get down from this tree. Would you be willing to help carry me down?"

"No way!" cried Manjo. "You may be very clever, but I'm not foolish. I'll not give you a chance to eat me."

"No, no, no," assured the crocodile, "you are mistaken. I have no desire to eat you. Didn't I already tell you that I enjoy being the first to do things? I want to be the first crocodile ever to be helped by a human. Then, I will also be the first crocodile ever to show kindness to a human."

Once Manjo understood the crocodile's situation, he didn't hesitate to help. He climbed up the tree next to the crocodile's side. It wasn't easy, but he managed to get the animal across his back. The crocodile's head rested on Manjo's right shoulder and chest while the tail draped over his left shoulder and down to his knees.

The animal felt heavy and cold. At one point, Manjo almost fell. Carefully, slowly, the two made it to the ground. Manjo was near exhaustion, but it was the crocodile who complained of being tired.

"Oh, Manjo," begged the crocodile, "please don't put me down here. Please carry me to the river. I feel a little sick. Please place me in the water. It'll refresh me."

Manjo stumbled on over to the water's edge. He was about to set the crocodile down, when he heard, "Oh, Manjo, please take me out a little way into the water. I'm so tired. It will help me so much."

Manjo didn't want to get his clothes wet, but he wanted to help the crocodile. He placed his shoes and gun on the shore and waded into the water, knee-deep, then waist-deep.

"If I go any farther, the water will cover my head," said Manjo.

"You have been very kind to me. This is an excellent spot. You may put me down here."

"Very well, my friend, I will visit you tomorrow."

"No, I don't think that will be possible," snapped the crocodile.

"But why not?" asked the hunter.

"Because I plan to eat you today!"

"What do you mean? You said you wanted to be the first crocodile to show kindness to a human! You said you like to be the first to do things," argued Manjo.

"Well," replied the crocodile with a grin, "I am the first crocodile to have ever been helped by a human. That's enough for today. I don't want to be the first foolish crocodile!"

The crocodile's friendly smile disappeared as he pulled Manjo under the water.

Wait a second! What just happened? No "happily ever after" for this very kind human? How can the bad guy - or crocodile - win in the end? Well, frequently in Liberian folk tales, the dirty rotten scoundrel learns his lesson in the end, and it's usually learned the hard way. But, sometimes, that scoundrel gets away with being dirty and rotten. If you prefer a "happily ever after" version, fortunately, there is another ending to this tale. Let's just skip back a few paragraphs and read on.

"Oh, Manjo," begged the crocodile, "please don't put me down here. Please carry me to the river. I feel a little sick. Please place me in the water. It'll refresh me."

Manjo stumbled on over to the water's edge, about to set the crocodile down, when he heard, "Oh, Manjo, please take me out a little ways into the water. I'm so tired. It will help me so much."

Now Manjo had an extremely kind heart, as we all know, but he also had a very wise brain. He wasn't about to set foot in any river with a crocodile. His mama didn't raise a fool. Instead of dipping his feet in the water, he stepped high upon a large rock. Then, with all his might, he tossed that crafty crocodile into the river. However, Manjo was all worn out, and that crocodile was so huge! Manjo couldn't throw him far at all. And, that might have been a good thing. The crocodile's head hit that rock, and it stunned him for a little bit. It gave Manjo enough time to get to a safe distance.

"Why did you do that?" snapped the crocodile.

"Because I know what you would have done if we were in deep water!"

"Well, you can't blame a crocodile for trying. You know, it would have made me famous. The first crocodile to ever trick a human."

"Listen well, Crocodile," warned Manjo. "If I ever see you in a tree again, it's going to be time for target practice. And, I'm a good hunter!" Just to emphasize his point, Manjo aimed and shot just to the side of the crocodile's right ear. Before a second shot could be fired, the old scoundrel quickly slid into the water's depths. Nobody ever saw him up in any tree ever again.

And, yes, Manjo lived happily ever after.

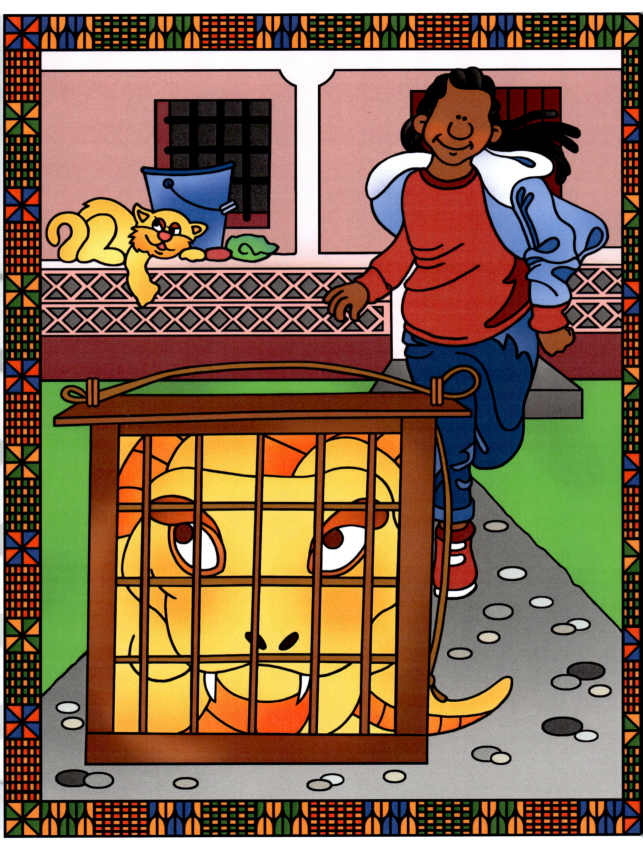

ONE MAN'S TROUBLE

"Rats! Rats!" cried the chief's wife in disgust. "Our village has too many rats! They spoil the rice."

"They spoil everything and they are everywhere!" cried the chief. "They destroy the cassava patch! They even disturb my sleep. I must get them out of my village."

And, since that's what the chief wanted, that's just what the chief did. He ordered the villagers to make rat traps. Traps were placed on all the paths leading to the village. They were set on the farms, in the attics of houses, under people's beds and around the streams. Any place a rat could be found, the villagers were ordered to place a trap. Everyone was pleased about the solution to the problem - well, almost everyone.

Cat seemed to be the only one in the village who was upset with the chief's command. "These traps are such a problem! Now I don't have a chance to catch any food," he cried. "The people destroy the rats after they catch them, and I am left with nothing to eat. I will starve if these traps remain in the village! My family will starve as well."

He needed help and he needed it immediately. To solve this problem, Cat went to his neighbors. "My dear friend, Cow," pleaded Cat, "help me destroy these traps. If I don't get rid of them right away, I will die of hunger."

"Rats are very disgusting creatures," mooed the cow. "I don't like them. I don't want them in my feed bin. I am quite happy that we now have these traps. Yes, I want the traps here. This is not my problem. You need to deal with it."

In desperation, Cat went to his other neighbor, Goat. He begged, "Please, help me destroy these traps, my friend. My family and I are so hungry. My children are starving."

"I am not going to help you with this problem," bleated the goat. "I only eat grass and rice. I think maybe you should try that as well. Anyway, this is not my problem. You need to deal with it."

Chicken was no more help than the other neighbors when Cat cried, "Oh, help me destroy all of these traps. I'm suffering. I am really suffering. Please, help me."

"Why should I care about silly old traps?" clucked Chicken. "I have no concern for cats or rats. This is not my problem. You need to deal with it and learn to take care of yourself."

So Cat's neighbors did nothing to help him in his time of suffering. And, he and his family certainly suffered. All by himself, Cat tried to destroy the traps, but there were just too many. They were everywhere. He knew that unless help came soon, very soon, he and his family would perish. The poor cat was desperate.

Help came, and it came in a very unexpected way.

One day a snake passed behind the chief's house, and the little treat he saw in a trap caught his eye. Of course, he had no idea it was a rat trap. All he cared about was the treat. And the trap worked exactly as it was supposed to work. The snake was captured.

And, he wasn't happy at all.

No matter how he wiggled and squirmed, the snake could not escape from the trap. The more he struggled, the more vexed he became. And, he was extremely vexed.

When the chief's only daughter came out the back door of his home, she spied the snake in the trap. "Mr. Snake," she said, "what are you doing in there? That's a trap only for rats."

The angry snake saw no humor in the situation. And, he certainly had no patience for a little girl. He bit her!

And she died instantly!

Of course, this broke the chief's heart. The little girl was his only daughter. He was so upset that he had ever ordered the traps to be made. "Which is worse," he cried, "to have rats or to lose a daughter?"

"Get rid of all these traps," he ordered. "Destroy every one of them. All of the traps must go. I do not want any other family to suffer the same misfortune. Get rid of those traps now!"

With the destruction of the rat traps, Cat's problems were over. Instantly! But the troubles for his neighbors just began. A feast was ordered to honor the chief's only daughter. "Kill the cow, the goat and the chicken," ordered the chief. "This must be a grand feast to honor my lost child."

The villagers quickly captured the animals as the chief instructed. Cat's three neighbors were tied together and herded to the center of the village as preparations for the feast took place all around them. Cook fires blazed as palm oil bubbled. Village women pounded rice in mortars while little girls gathered supplies for different soups. It was to be a feast that everyone would remember for many years to come because the chief's daughter was loved by all.

Cat, now with a very full belly, heard the commotion in the village. It's said that curiosity killed the cat, but that wasn't going to happen this day. And, as he strolled through the village, he happened to pass by his neighbors.

"Oh, our friend," sobbed the three animals, "come rescue us! Please come set us free. The chief wants to kill us for a feast. You must rescue us, Cat."

"Where were you when my family was perishing?" asked the cat. "If you had helped destroy the traps, none of you would now be facing this death. I am afraid I can only give you the same words you had for me. 'This is not my problem. You need to deal with it.' "

Cat turned around and left them to return to his family. The three neighbors realized - and too late - that one man's trouble is every man's trouble.

SENGBE AND THE FISHING RULES

The town chief had a terrible night of sleep. He tossed and turned with dreams about genies chasing him. Why did they want him? Why were they after him? The fitful sleep continued. Eventually, the genies captured him in his dream.

"What do you want from me?" cried the chief.

"We have come to give you an important message. The river that flows near your village belongs to us. We have permitted your people to fish in it while there was plenty of fish. However, that is no longer the case. You must give the people rules to limit their fishing in the river."

"But what shall we eat?" asked the chief.

"There are other rivers with fish," replied the genies. "The people should also fish there. Follow the rules that we will give you and your village will have no problems."

The chief awoke with a jolt. Was this a dream or did the genies really come to speak with him? He couldn't be sure. He did know he had four rules in mind for fishing. Had the genies given him these rules? He quickly wrote the rules down before going back to sleep.

In the morning, the new rules for fishing in the river were announced to the villagers. Some people mumbled because it would be harder to get fish. Others scoffed because they didn't believe in genies. Everyone, however, took the rules seriously because they knew their chief meant what he said.

"All people must follow these rules or face my punishment and the possible revenge of the genies."

Sengbe carefully copied down all the rules that the chief gave the people and took them home to study. He set his mind to work. He knew there must be a way to still fish in the river and not break the rules. He determined that he would find that way.

The four rules were very clear. Even the youngest child found them easy to understand.

Rule 1. Men must fish with a net.

Rule 2. Women must fish with a hook.

Rule 3. Men and women may only fish in the river when it is raining.

Rule 4. After catching the fish, they must be given to a person from another town.

Sengbe studied the rules carefully and realized that he could fish all he wanted in the river if he followed the rules exactly. While others in the village suffered without fresh fish, Sengbe had plenty. The neighbors grew concerned that Sengbe had broken the rules. They didn't want to face the chief's punishment or the genies' revenge. It was decided that Sengbe must be brought to the chief for investigation.

"These are serious charges brought against you, Sengbe," warned the chief. "How do you plead?"

"I am innocent of breaking any of the rules. I have followed all of the rules exactly."

"You have been seen fishing with a pole. This is against the rules. What do you have to say for yourself?"

"I say it is not against the rules, my chief. The rule states we men must fish with a net. It doesn't say we can't fish with a net and a pole at the same time."

"But the net never gets wet!" cried a neighbor woman. "It's just tied to the end of your pole!"

"When I fish with a pole, it also never gets wet."

The chief understood that Sengbe had cleverly followed this rule. Although Sengbe had not actually broken the rule, he still could vex the genies with his craftiness.

"Sengbe," continued the chief, "it is said that you have been fishing when it is not raining. This is another serious charge against you. Is it true?"

"Yes and no, Chief," admitted Sengbe. "The rules say we must only fish when it is raining. It doesn't say where it must be raining. In the dry season, when there are no rains, our river stops completely. But now the river is high. It must be raining somewhere to provide this water. As you can see, again, I am following the rules exactly."

The chief agreed with Sengbe's logic. The rules didn't say exactly where it had to be raining. Again, the chief could not charge Sengbe with breaking the rules, but he wondered if the genies would be as understanding.

"The final charge is that you are catching the fish and not giving them to someone from another village," said the chief. "How do you explain this charge?"

"Everyone knows my brother lives in the village across the river," replied Sengbe. "I always give the fish to him but, when he cooks them, he shares the meal with me."

"But your brother has been staying with you for the past four months!" cried the same neighbor woman. "That makes him one of us. He's not from the other village."

"Woman," glared Sengbe, "when you went to visit your son in the city last year for six months, where did you tell people you lived? Did you say you lived in our village or the city?"

The woman bowed her head and mumbled, "The village."

"There, so you see, Chief," beamed Sengbe, "I have followed each rule exactly. I have broken no rules and can be charged with no wrong."

"I see there is nothing we can do to charge you for your actions, but you may be too clever for your own good," warned the chief. "I'm sure you have angered the genies. They will not forget this. For your own safety, do not go to the river."

"I will continue to do exactly as I have been doing," said Sengbe. "All of you admit I have the law on my side. I've done nothing wrong."

The next day, the village had a terrible rain storm. A little wet weather wasn't going to prevent Sengbe from fishing down at the river. When the chief saw Sengbe leaving town, he was relieved that the man was at least following one of the rules. It definitely was raining at the river that day. Sengbe sat down on the bridge to prepare his pole and net. He never saw the high wave of rushing water that hit the bridge and swept it away.

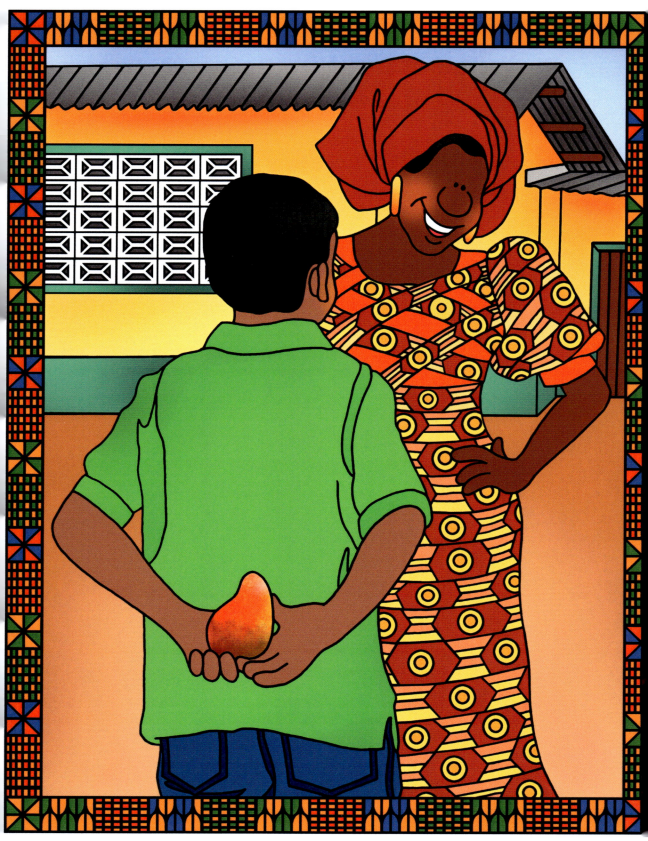

SIXTEEN PLUMS

"I have just seen the most beautiful plums on the walk I took, Mother," cried the small boy. "There was an entire grove of trees, and it was filled with ripe plums. "

"And where was this mysterious grove with all the ripe plums, my son?" asked the mother.

"Oh, it's far from here," replied the boy. "I took the path until it came to a spot where I must either go left or right. I turned right. Next, I turned left and then I took two more right turns. After the final right turn, I found the grove of trees."

Much to the boy's surprise, his mother replied, "I know all about that special grove. Now, tell me, did you happen to see any old men on your walk?"

"Now that you mention it, Mother, I did. There was one old man near each of the four intersections that I came upon," he answered.

"I thought so. These four brothers guard that beautiful plum grove," explained the mother. "They never let anyone take the plums. I know those plums look so tempting, but nobody ever takes any of them. Those men will beat anyone who tries to get them."

"I can't believe those four brothers could be so very selfish," cried the young boy. There were plenty of plums for everyone. "Why couldn't they share?" he wondered.

"No one really knows why they don't share those plums," replied the mother. "They have never done that, and it's my guess that they never will."

"Well, I'm going to tell them how rude they are," announced the small boy. "I'm going to the grove for some plums right now. Someone needs to teach them how to share."

The mother just smiled. She never dreamed for one moment that her son really intended to go back to the grove and confront those men. She just thought it was big talk from her small boy.

The four brothers never disturbed the boy on his first walk because he didn't carry any of their precious plums. At each intersection, as he walked back to the grove, the boy waved as he passed by. Still, none of the brothers spoke to him, although they were a bit surprised to have anyone wave at them.

The boy marched into the grove and carefully selected sixteen plums for his basket. He placed the basket on his head and then turned around for his long walk home. It didn't take long to reach the oldest brother at the first intersection.

"Who are you, boy?" boomed the brother. "How dare you take my plums! Didn't your parents ever teach you about stealing? Give them to me now, or I will beat you."

"Didn't your parents ever teach you about manners? How can you be so selfish and rude?" demanded the small boy. "My mother taught me to share. Didn't your mother teach you anything?"

The words embarrassed the brother. He didn't know how to respond. How could such a small boy speak to him like that? It had never happened before.

"As I said, my mother taught me to share. I won't give you all of my plums, but I will give you half of them," said the small boy. "Here, take these eight plums, and I'll keep the other eight for myself."

The small boy's words made sense to the brother. He took the eight plums and let the boy pass on his way down the path. The man shook his head when the boy left. Nothing like that had ever happened to him before. Nobody had ever talked to him about sharing.

The small boy continued on his journey home until he came upon the second intersection. The same thing happened. The next brother ran out yelling at the little boy. "What are you doing with my plums? Do you want me to beat you?"

Again, the small boy scolded the brother for being selfish and rude. "I'm willing to share the plums equally with you. Here, you can have four, and I'll take the other four."

The puzzled man agreed and took four plums. Nothing like this had ever happened before.

Once again, the small boy continued on his journey, this time with four plums. Again, at the third intersection, another one of the brothers threatened the small boy. "Rogue! Thief! Why have you taken my plums? I will beat you if you don't return them."

And, once again, the child scolded the older man. "Why are you so selfish when we both know it is better to share? Let's divide the plums. We both can have two of them."

Once more, the brother was so confused by this child's words that he also agreed. Just like his brothers, he shook his head because it had never happened before.

Finally, the small boy came to the last intersection. One last time, he was confronted by the last of the brothers. One last time, the boy scolded the man for his selfishness. "You little rogue! Give me back my plums. Give them now, or I will beat you."

And, one last time, the child scolded the selfish man. "Don't you know it is always better to share? I will give you one of my plums, and I will keep the other."

One last time, the boy was allowed to pass, with one plum in his basket. Of course, he left the last brother shaking his head just like the other three brothers. It had never happened before.

When the small boy returned home, he presented the plum to his mother.

"Where did you get this plum?" she asked in amazement.

"I told you I was going to get a plum from the grove," declared the small boy.

"But nobody has been able to do that before!" cried the mother. "You are a clever son."

"Well, I may be clever, but you taught me how to share."

When the mother and child finished eating the plum, the small boy carefully planted the seed. He planned to start his own plum grove. His grove would be different, however, because everyone in his village would be welcome to enjoy his plums.

SPIDER'S SMILE

"My good friend, Spider," clucked Chicken, "I think your problem is you can't be satisfied with what you have."

"What do you mean?" asked Spider.

"If someone has something that you do not possess, you cannot rest until you also own the same thing," replied Chicken.

"Ouch! That maybe a little too honest, but I think it is true," said Spider. "But how can I possibly be happy when all my friends have lovely white teeth, and I have no teeth at all? Really, I'm the only one who doesn't have any teeth."

"Excuse me . . . Not all of your friends have teeth," answered Chicken. "Have you forgotten me? I don't have teeth, and I am very happy just the way I am."

"Well, I'm not," cried Spider. "You said you had a plan to get me some teeth. So, out with it. What's your brilliant plan? I just have to have that smile."

Chicken led Spider to her farm behind the house. Now Chicken knew how to grow an abundant farm. She had so many melons growing there - melons with lots of seeds. Seeds that could be bleached white in the sun. Spider immediately understood his friend's plan. "I think it's a stroke of genius," beamed the delighted spider.

The two friends collected some seeds, washed them in the stream, dried them in the sun and prepared a set of false teeth for Spider. A happier spider could be found nowhere. He was now the proud owner of a white set of teeth - for both upper and lower jaws - and he could not stop smiling.

"This is too wonderful to believe!" exclaimed Spider. "We must have a big party to celebrate. I want everyone to see my new white smile. Oh! There's so much to do. I must prepare rice and soup. I must tap palm wine. I must make invitations for all the guests. Where do I begin? There's so much to do!"

"I'll help you take care of everything, my friend. Don't worry about the party. But, there is also one other thing you must do," cautioned Chicken. "Add it to the top of your list."

"What's that?" asked Spider.

"You must be careful to take excellent care of your new teeth. You must clean them every night before you go to bed. If you don't do that, they will spoil."

"That's no problem at all," chuckled Spider. "I'll be happy to do that. Every night! Always. Now, I must borrow a large pot to boil my rice. Maybe my neighbor will have one?"

The party was a grand feast. Spider could not stop smiling as everyone admired his new teeth. There was plenty of music, just the right amount of food and maybe too much palm wine. Spider could barely keep his eyes open when the party ended, and it was time for bed. What a great party it had been! Everyone agreed.

It didn't take long for Spider to fall asleep. He was in bed as soon as his last guest left. And, you can guess what he forgot to do.

Not long after Spider fell asleep, Ant strolled past Spider's house. There was simply no way for Ant to miss the wonderful smells that came from the home. Ant loved party smells. There are always crumbs and treats scattered around the floor after parties. It was too much temptation for a poor ant to resist. Honestly, he never could resist any temptation related to food.

First, Ant knocked gently on the door, but no one answered. He called out to Spider, but there was no reply. He knocked on the door a little louder. "Spider, are you in there? What smells so good? Let me in," begged the Ant.

Finally, when he discovered that the front door was not locked, Ant opened the door and just let himself into Spider's house. He had to find out what smelled so delicious. He really had no choice.

The hungry ant searched all the usual places. He peeked under the table, around the chairs and in the kitchen. There were certainly some interesting smells, but not the one that lured him into the house with that wonderful aroma. "Where was that coming from?" he asked himself.

Ant couldn't really ask Spider. He was still asleep. But then, Spider opened his mouth and let out a loud snore. Ant not only heard the snore, but he smelled it. Yes, the smell that attracted the ant that night was inside Spider's mouth. That's right. Those teeth attracted Ant with an aroma he just could not resist. Spider had ignored Chicken's warning. He went to bed without cleaning his teeth. He was so tired he just forgot to do what everyone knows needs to be done every evening.

Ant simply couldn't help himself.

He crept up to Spider. Carefully, he plucked a melon seed from his mouth. It was every bit as good as he had imagined, maybe even a little bit better.

Then, before he was caught, Ant slipped out of Spider's home. When he returned to his hill, he had quite an adventure to tell his friends and family. The idea of eating such tasty melon seeds as well as a little adventure interested all of the other ants. They quietly returned to Spider's home. One by one, they didn't stop feasting until all of the melon seeds were eaten. The ants all agreed that the spider's new teeth were very, very tasty.

In the morning, Chicken came over to Spider's house to tell him how much she enjoyed the party. "Oh, Spider," clucked Chicken, "the party was terrific, and your teeth are just . . . just . . . ."

"Wonderful?" asked the spider.

"No, gone! Your teeth are all gone!" exclaimed Chicken.

Spider ran to the mirror in horror. Sure enough, every single melon seed was gone. To Chicken's amazement, Spider did not cry. He looked at his friend and declared, "Maybe I was not meant to have those teeth after all. They were a lot of work, and I forgot to clean them last night after the party."

Chicken could not believe her ears! Well, that is, if chickens have ears.

"I think I'm happy with myself just the way I am," said the spider with a smile.

Chicken thought it was a beautiful smile.

TALE OF TWO NEIGHBORS

The hunger season usually frustrated Turtle. He always seemed to have enough for himself, but his family and friends always begged from him.

"My man, have you got money so I can buy my rice?" asked Turtle's brother.

"Do you have any pepper I could borrow today?" begged his sister.

"Please give me some palm nuts," pleaded his neighbor.

Turtle did not enjoy sharing at all. One day he complained about this to Hawk. "Everyone always humbugs me for everything I own, and I do not like it one bit. I'm so very tired of having family so close."

"I understand completely what you're talking about," said Hawk. "When I hunt in the bush, I always eat my food far from home. If I bring meat home, so many members of my family want it that I don't even get a bone!"

"It's good to meet someone who thinks like me," replied Turtle with a smile. "We should move deep into the bush, far from our begging families. We could live in peace where no one would ever again ask us for anything."

Hawk liked this idea immediately, so the two friends made their plans. The next day they told their friends and families that they were going on a hunting trip. It was almost the truth. They were hunting for a new place to live. They left their village never to return again.

The journey was especially hard for Turtle since he could not fly. After days of searching, the two friends came upon a clearing. There was a huge bug-a-bug hill where Hawk could build a nest and plenty of level ground for Turtle's home. The friends knew that their search was over. They finally found a new place to live.

The two friends were quite happy for months. Each did as he pleased and never disturbed the other. When Hawk caught an animal to eat, he never shared it with Turtle. When Turtle prepared a fine meal, he never offered Hawk an invitation. It was exactly the kind of life each of them wanted.

But all this harmony ended the day Hawk ran out of salt. He flew down to his neighbor and asked, "Turtle, please give me some salt. Mine is finished, and I need a small amount."

"No! No! No!" cried Turtle. "You must take care of yourself. I did not move all the way out here to have you humbug me. Get your own salt!"

Turtle wasn't finished either. He built a fence around his yard. He knew Hawk could easily fly over the fence, but he also knew Hawk would understand the purpose of the fence. No visitors allowed! No begging! No one welcome!

Of course, Hawk's feelings were hurt.

He thought about Turtle's behavior and decided to teach him a lesson. A few days later, he invited Turtle to his home for supper.

"Hmm . . ." wondered Turtle. "All these months we've lived here and Hawk has never invited me to his home. He's doing this to shame me because I didn't give him any salt. Well, it will not work. I do not shame that easily. I'll go to his house and eat the meal. But, in the future, that clever hawk will still never get any salt from me."

Turtle began what was for him a long climb to the top of the bug-a-bug hill where Hawk's nest was located. The hill was covered with sticky palm oil which made climbing difficult. Turtle slipped and slid down the hill making little progress.

"What's keeping you?" called Hawk. "The food is getting cold. I hope you don't mind that I begin eating."

Turtle struggled on the hill. Finally, he cried out, "Why is all this oil on your hill? Did you pour it here just to make things difficult for me?"

"Of course, I would do no such thing," replied Hawk. "Earlier today, I spilled a pan of hot oil when I removed it from the fire. I even burned myself, but don't worry. I am fine now. Please hurry and come eat with me."

Turtle did not believe one word of this. He knew the oil was wasted on the hill especially to prevent his climb. He continued slipping and climbing until Hawk finally called out, "I'm sorry you didn't want to join me for supper. The food was so delicious, but I've eaten all of it. Maybe you'll eat with me some other time?"

Completely covered with mud and palm oil, the hungry turtle returned to his home. He would not forgive this insult, and he certainly would not forget it. He would not sleep until he had a plan to teach Hawk a lesson he would never forget.

Very early in the morning, well before Hawk was awake, Turtle set his trap. And later that same day, he called to his neighbor. "Hawk, I am so sorry that I was late for supper last night. You were right to eat without me. I promise that I will not be late the next time. Will you please come eat with me today?"

Hawk could not believe his ears. - And, who knew hawks had ears? - He thought, "When I leave this turtle alone, he never calls on me. When I treat the guy badly, he invites me to his house. This is one very strange turtle. I wonder what he will do if I treat him well?" Of course, Hawk could not pass up a dinner invitation. But, what would that foolish turtle prepare?

Hawk flew down to his neighbor's front gate. Turtle graciously welcomed him into the yard. And, the moment Hawk stepped through the gate, the trap sprung, and he found himself hanging helplessly upside down in the air.

"What happened? Why am I upside down? What's wrong?" cried Hawk.

"Oh, nothing is wrong," snapped the turtle. "But you were wrong to treat me so poorly yesterday."

"That was just a misunderstanding. What are you doing, Turtle?"

"There is no misunderstanding today, Hawk. I am sharpening my knife."

"B-b-b-but, w-w-w-why are you putting water in the very large pot?"

"My friend, I have a lot of cooking to do."

"What are you going to prepare? Chicken? Deer?"

"No, no, nothing like that. I want something very delicious. I want something like YOU!"

With those words spoken, Turtle grabbed the knife and killed the hawk. He cut him up in small pieces and threw him in the pot to boil. Turtle continued his preparations. When he smelled the meat burning in the pot, he couldn't remember how much water he used. "Did I pour in two pans or three? I better check on that," he thought.

The pot was very tall, too tall to see over. Turtle needed his bamboo step ladder. Then, he climbed on the edge of the pot with a container of water carefully balanced on his head. Once on top of the pot, he looked down inside.

And, that's when he slipped.

Turtle fell into the pot with the pan of water on top of him. He was trapped inside the pot. As it turned out, there was plenty of water to cook both the hawk and the turtle very well.

THE REAL REASON SPIDER HAS A SMALL WAIST

"What's wrong with you today?" asked the merchant as Spider walked into his store. "You don't look well at all. Do you have a fever? Is it very high?"

"No, I don't have a fever," replied Spider.

"That's too bad, my friend. I have some excellent medicine for fevers. Are you sure you don't have a fever?"

"Just leave me alone," grumbled the spider. "I repeat, leave me alone."

Spider was obviously in a bad mood. Not only did he treat the merchant rudely, but he didn't even greet the others gathered around the store. There was a turtle sitting on a rock, a dog resting in the corner with a bone and a complete stranger near the entrance.

Spider's behavior vexed Turtle. "We didn't come to you," he scolded. "You, Spider, came to where we were in this store. Why are you treating us so rudely?"

"Be careful with this spider," cautioned the stranger. "I know all about his cleverness. If you aren't careful, you may fall for one of his tricks for he is a crafty one. But, today I think he's just hungry. Spider, let me buy you a drink."

"I asked you to leave me alone! " repeated Spider. "And, that's what I mean. I'm sick, so leave me alone."

"Do you have a cold?" asked the merchant. "I also have new medicine for colds. You would be my first customer to buy it. Would you like some cold medicine?"

"I think he's hurting because he finally ate too much," chuckled the turtle. "Is your stomach too full?"

"You are so wrong," cried Spider. "You're all so very wrong. I am hurting because my waist is so small. It has been hurting me for such a long time."

"Tell us, why is your waist so small? There must be a good reason for this. Could you explain what's going on with you?" asked the stranger. "We really want to know."

"I might be able to tell you the story if I had some bread to eat," replied Spider.

The stranger put a few coins on the counter, and the merchant handed Spider some freshly baked bread. He eagerly ate a few bites before he began his story. Everyone waited anxiously to hear what he had to say.

"Four years ago, I attended a feast."

"Ha! I knew it had something to do with food," interrupted the merchant. "Spider stories are usually about food."

Spider ignored the comment and continued. "As I said, four years ago I attended a feast. It was deep in the bush where people rarely ever go. As it started getting dark, I decided I better head for home. It's not easy to walk in the bush when it is dark. And, it became dark before I got home. It was hard to see, but I could hear something, someone, behind me. I tried to walk faster, but I heard the noise behind me move faster as well."

"Suddenly, Leopard jumped out and attacked me!"

"He put his strong arms around my waist and squeezed as hard as he could. That old leopard was strong, but I fought with eight arms and legs. We fought all night long, and he never let go of my waist. It was his strong grip that made my waist so small."

"Leopard never would have let go if I hadn't caught him in my web. Yes, my friends, thank goodness I thought clearly enough to do that. I tied up that cat, and then I killed him with my cutlass. If you come to my house, you can see the leopard skin."

"Is that so?" asked the dog getting up from his corner.

"Yes, that's exactly how it happened," replied Spider. "If you will please excuse me now, I really must go."

Spider quickly left the store without another word.

The dog turned around to face the others. "You know he would never have told such a story if he had seen me sitting in the corner. It was a good story, but it's just absolutely not true. Trust me, not one word of it is true."

"And, you know the true story about his narrow waist?" asked the merchant. He pulled up his stool ready for another good tale. "Please share it with us."

"Well, I should know all about it. After all, I was there when it happened," said the dog. "Yes, someone squeezed Spider's waist, but it wasn't any old leopard. It was me. Yes, man's best friend, not necessarily spider's best friend."

"This could be interesting," said the stranger. "Merchant, let's have some cold drinks for everyone here while we listen to this version of the story."

"Thank you," said Dog. "Now, as I was saying, a few years ago Spider and I made the mistake of making our farm together. It was not a wise thing to do since Spider always tricks everyone. And, anyone who ever makes a farm with Spider always ends up regretting it. Always. Anyway, we agreed to the project and that each day our wives would take turns cooking for us."

"I knew it!" declared the merchant. "This story also has something to do with food."

"Yes, it certainly does," continued Dog. "On the first day, Spider's wife cooked the food. She put in too much pepper for me. My mouth was on fire and I needed to get some water. When I went to the river, Spider ate all of the food. We got into a big palaver over that, and I squeezed his waist as hard as I could. It was the first and last day of our farming together."

"Well, now we have two good stories," said the stranger with a smile, "but how do we know which one is the truth?"

"Obviously, I spoke the truth," barked the dog. "Didn't you see how quickly Spider left as soon as he saw me. I tell you, he was too ashamed to say another word. He had to get out of the store."

"Enough of this!" snapped the turtle. "I've known Spider since before you were born. His tricks go way back. And unfortunately, I go way back too. But after Spider pulled a trick on me, I decided to teach him a lesson. And, he remembers it every time he sees his narrow waist."

"Let me guess, it has something to do with food?" asked the merchant.

"Naturally," answered Turtle. "I, too, made the mistake of farming with Spider. I may have been the first one to make that mistake. Everyone knows Spider is a lousy partner for a farm project. I had no idea at the time. Well, every day during harvest time he ran to the farm and told me the devil was coming. In absolute terror, I ran in the bush to hide while Spider harvested the rice for himself. When I realized what Spider was doing, I said nothing because I had my own plans for that clever trickster. I invited him to have rice at my house."

The merchant turned to the stranger and said, "Turtle lives under the water down at the river. The rains sometimes wash away his pots. That's why he came here today."

"Well, I knew that Spider couldn't come under water to eat at my house," said the turtle with a grin. "Spiders are not heavy enough to sink. My wife prepared a fine feast. She makes excellent beans gravy, and we thoroughly enjoyed it while Spider sat at the river's edge and cried. Finally, Spider tied some rocks to a string and wrapped the string around his waist.

This enabled him to come down to my house. But, by the time he arrived, all the food was eaten. His small waist is a continual reminder that one time I tricked him instead of the other way around."

"That's a third fine story, but tell me, who do we believe?" asked the merchant.

"Why, me, of course," snapped Turtle. "After Spider told his story, he noticed me sitting on this rock. When he saw me pointing to it, that's when he became embarrassed and had to leave. He knew I was all too aware of the real truth."

"This is all very interesting to me," confessed the stranger, "but I have to tell you that you are all misinformed. Spider's small waist was the result of a visit to my town. When he saw the rope I used to tie up my bundle, he remembered the truth about his waist and ran away. The people of my town once tied up Spider's waist very tightly when he came to our feast."

"And here we are with another story about food," interrupted the merchant.

"Yes, allow me to tell you my version of the tale," begged the stranger. "Normally, visitors are welcome in my town. The only exception is when we have feasts. Usually, guests are given the best foods, nice beds and extremely warm welcomes. However, during times of feasts, a stranger may actually be beaten or even killed. It's our custom. It's our law. Nothing is going to change it, so strangers just need to be warned."

"That's a law that could get Spider in trouble," said the merchant. "He cannot resist a good feast."

"Exactly," replied the stranger. "When Spider came to my father's house, we hid him in the attic and warned him to stay there. Of course, we told him what might happen if anyone in the village saw him. The warning didn't work. He tore a hole in the thatch roof and climbed down to the celebration. He tried to get some food when the women cooking were not watching. But, he was caught. Just like I told you, the town people tied a rope to his waist and attached it to two palm trees. The rope was pulled tight and Spider was beaten. The more he struggled, the more the rope was pulled tighter and tighter. That's why Spider has such a small waist today. That's the real reason."

"Well, the way I heard it," said the merchant, "there were two feasts. Spider was invited to both of them, but they were the same afternoon in different villages. Such a dilemma for Spider! He didn't know which village would first be ready, so Spider tied two ropes to his waist. Each rope went to one of the villages where one of the feasts was to be held. When the food was ready, a gentle tug on the rope would signal Spider, and he would come to eat. Unfortunately for Spider, both meals were ready at exactly the same time. Spider was trapped in the middle when both ropes were pulled. And, it seems that they were pulled very hard. That's why his waist is so small."

"Whichever story is true really doesn't matter, I guess," said the turtle.

"I agree," replied the stranger, "but it has made for an interesting afternoon. Thank you all for the stories. I must hurry home for a feast in my town tonight. I would invite you all, but you know what would happen to you there."

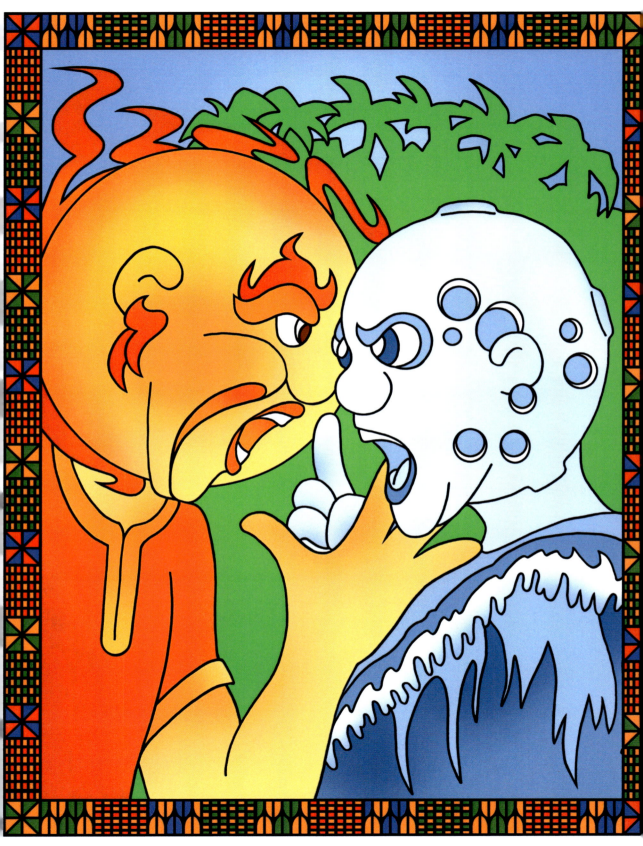

THE SUN'S DAILY SEARCH

Long ago when the sun and moon lived in a small village, people didn't need to search the sky to find them. The sun worked on his rice farm with all the other men. The moon sold her vegetables in town at the market with the women. Their children, the stars, played in the village with all the kids in the neighborhood.

One beautiful morning the moon decided to go for a little walk. "I'll only be gone for a few minutes. I need to get some fresh air."

"That's fine. Take your time, but don't be too long," warned the sun. "I don't want you to be late in preparing my lunch."

"I'll be back in plenty of time for that," beamed the moon. "Don't let your stomach worry at all."

But it was such a beautiful day that the moon soon forgot all about the time. There were too many colorful flowers to pick, too many birds to hear and too many songs to sing. Not only did she forget about lunch, but she was also late for supper.

Although the moon had a delightful day, there was a disaster waiting for her at home. The sun wasn't just mad; he was extremely vexed! "Where is that wife of mine?" he roared. "I've been hungry for entirely too long! And, the kids! They have cried all afternoon. All afternoon! Nonstop! Let me repeat, all afternoon!"

The sun lost all his patience long before lunch was supposed to be served. By the time the moon finally appeared, supper was late as well. And, the children continued crying.

The moon's beautiful mood ended when the sun screamed one complaint after another.

"Where have you been all day?"
"The children are hungry."
"They have been crying for hours."
"I am nearly starved!"
"How could you do this to us?"
"Fix us some food right away!"
"Get busy and do your job!"

Nobody wants to be treated like that. Nobody wants to be treated without respect. The moon was no exception. The smile she had worn all day completely disappeared. She glared at the sun and shouted, "Fix it yourself! You are perfectly able to walk into the kitchen and prepare your own meal."

The sun was already mad, and his temper just flared. "You must not be hearing me correctly," he roared. "I said, 'Cook the food! That's your job!'"

"Who do you think you are talking to me like that?" asked the moon.

"I think I'm your starving husband!"

"You can't treat me this way."

"I think I just did," he cried.

"Don't you dare tell me what to do!"

"I will do whatever I feel like doing."

"Well, let me tell you. I am your wife - not your servant!"

"Well, wife, serve me something to eat!"

The terrible argument raged on as the children continued to cry. The sun wouldn't calm down, and the moon finally refused to speak to him. Nobody ate anything that night.

Nobody should go to bed angry. It's just not a good thing to do. Before the sun goes down, you should always settle your arguments. But, it appears that nobody told that to the sun or the moon. The moon was so angry that she couldn't sleep at all. Not one little wink. She went over and over the fight in her head. "How could the sun treat me that way?" she wondered. "That is not how a husband should treat a wife. And that is not how this husband is going to treat this wife!"

As she lay awake, she decided that the only thing she could do was leave. That very night she quietly gathered up the children and fled from the village. They raced across the sky to get as far away from the sun as possible.

When the sun awoke the next morning from a very deep sleep, he was much calmer. But when he looked for his wife, he discovered that his entire family had vanished. Right away, he realized that he had not behaved properly. "I should never have gotten so upset!" he thought.

But it was too late.

He rushed into the village looking for his family. "Old Woman," he cried, "have you seen my wife and children? Do you know what has happened to them or where they have gone?"

"I heard you last night, but I have not seen your family today," she replied.

No one in the village had seen them. No one could help the sun at all. They had no idea where his family was.

The sun searched across the sky looking for them. Whenever he found someone, he asked, "Have you seen my wife? Have you seen my children? Can you help me find my family?" No one was able to help him with his search.

All day, every day, the sun searched across the sky shining his light onto all the corners of the globe. He shined atop mountains and across oceans and deserts. He tried to reach into the deepest forests. He looked everywhere he could for his family.

During the day, while the sun searched the sky, the moon and the stars hid from him. He never found them. Every night, while the sun slept soundly, they came out of their hiding places.

The sun is still searching for them. Every day he continues to wander across the sky looking for his family. They are still hiding from him.

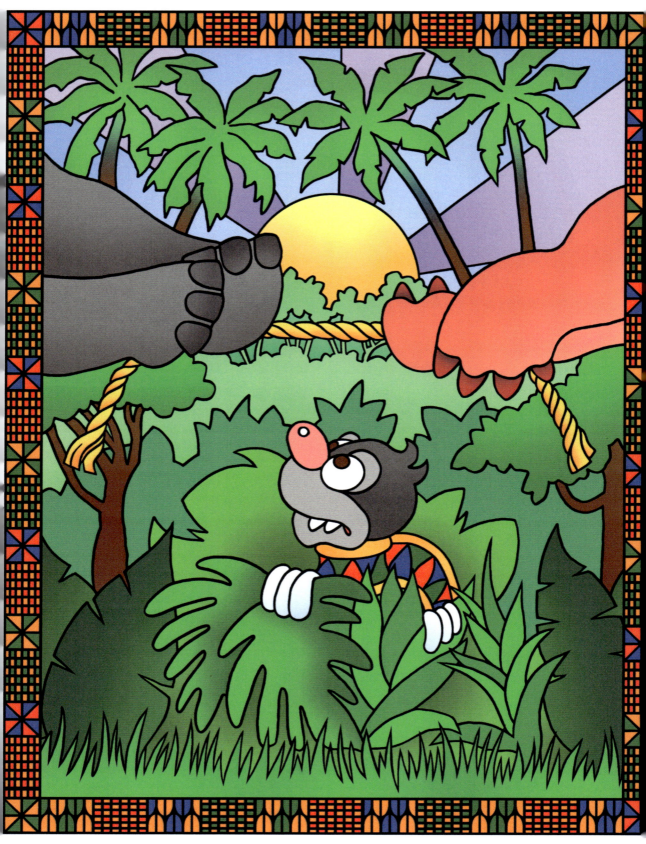

THE TUG OF WAR

"Elephant, I am tired of you saying I am weak," cried Spider. "You may be bigger than me, but I know the truth. I know I can beat you in a tug of war!"

"How can you possibly say such a thing?" snorted Elephant. "Even the flapping of my ear would send you flying. You can't be serious! There is no way you could ever beat me in a tug of war."

"I am serious about this. I know I'll win if you only give me a chance," challenged Spider. "Just take the rope and wrap it around your waist. I'll pull you over in no time."

"But I don't want to hurt you, my little friend. Something could go wrong if we do this. A tug of war between you and me would simply not be a fair contest," said Elephant.

"Well, I cannot agree with you on this. Please, let me at least try," pleaded the spider.

"Okay, if it will make you happy," agreed Elephant. "Help me get this rope wrapped around my waist."

"I'm so glad you are willing to do this," said Spider as he tightened the rope around his friend. "I am going to take my end of the rope down the hill a short distance. When I'm ready for the contest to begin, I will gently tug on the rope. That's the signal to begin the tug of war."

"I understand," said the elephant. "Well, I understand the rules, but I'm still not sure why we are doing this."

"Great, Elephant. This is going to be so much fun."

Spider quickly disappeared into the bush, but he did not prepare himself for the challenge. No, that crafty spider went looking for Hippo instead. "Hippo, my dear friend, I want to challenge you to a tug of war," said Spider.

"If you want to die, just tell me," laughed Hippo, "but don't try to involve me in a silly tug of war with you. There is just no way someone like you could ever beat me."

"You don't take me seriously," cried Spider. "I may be small, but I'm filled with muscle while you are big and all hot air. You can't beat me in this contest."

"Are you serious? Do you see how big I am?" asked Hippo. "Do you understand just how much muscle you're talking to?"

"You say muscle, but I hear mouse - a squeaky, little, terrified mouse," said Spider.

"Give me that rope," snorted Hippo. "It's time you have a squeaky little lesson on manners."

Spider gave him the end of the rope. As he helped tie the knot, the trickster instructed the hippo to wait until he went up the hill. "When I am ready for the tug of war to begin, I'll give the rope a gentle tug. That'll be the signal to start."

Spider traveled back up the hill and found a comfortable spot to relax, about halfway between Elephant and Hippo. He tugged on the rope and Elephant yanked with all his might. The force of the pull shocked Hippo at first. "How in the world did Spider do that?" he thought. But Hippo quickly regained his ground.

From where he sat, Spider saw both of the animals struggling. He certainly enjoyed the contest and absolutely had a very good laugh. He wasn't so sure his friends enjoyed the tug of war nearly as much. That didn't matter to Spider.

Hours passed. Spider actually fell asleep for a little while, but neither Elephant nor Hippo budged at all. Neither of them was prepared to lose to a spider. They'd never live that down.

"What is this?" thought Elephant. "How can something no bigger than a louse on my ear put up such a fight? Even if the entire spider population pulled on that rope, I should have won this contest a long while ago without breaking a sweat."

On the other end of the rope, Hippo wondered the very same thing. "Something tricky must be going on, and I know the trickster who would do this. I am not foolish, but I think I might have just been fooled."

At the same moment, both of the animals quit their struggle. Elephant stomped down the hill while Hippo stormed up, each determined to see how Spider could be so strong.

A few feet away from where Spider lay sleeping, the two animals saw each other, both of them still with the rope tied around the waist. They looked at the other in disbelief. And, they had the same question in mind. "Why are you at the other end of this rope?"

"Where is that Spider?" roared Elephant. "I'm going to crush him under my feet and then find some way to make him suffer!"

"Not if I find him first!" cried Hippo. "I'll boil him in palm oil!"

"He'll spend the rest of his days in prison!"

"I'll break every bone in his body!"
"He doesn't have any bones!"
"Okay, I'll tear him apart limb by limb!"
"I'll teach him a lesson he'll never forget!"
"That spider will never play another trick as long as he lives!"

While the two animals argued how they would torment Spider, the clever trickster awoke from his nap. Now, Spider was no fool. He knew the best thing to do was to get out of there as fast as possible. It was time to disappear for a while. He was far away from the hill by the time the two animals ended their plans for him. But, by then it was too late. They never found the clever spider.

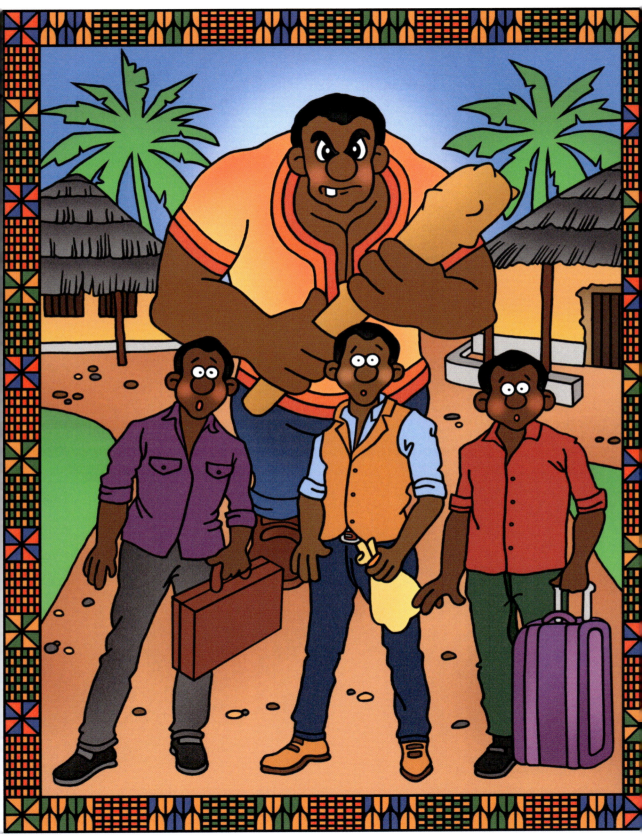

THREE BROTHERS WITH BAD HABITS

"I'm sorry, my sons, but this time you have just gone too far," said their father. "The elders have ordered me to send you from our village. You must leave today. The people are tired of your fighting, stealing and lying."

"But I was only fighting with the man because he accused my brother of stealing a chicken," cried the second brother.

"I did steal the chicken," admitted the first brother.

"Do you see what I mean?" asked the father. "The people are tired of all the problems you create. You know this is all your fault. We've all seen this coming for quite some time."

"Well, I am tired of these people too! I, for one, will be glad to leave this village," lied the third brother. "I plan to go to the big city to earn my fame and fortune. I don't need this little village and any of its bothersome people."

The three brothers had no choice. They packed all the belongings that they could carry and headed out of the village. Although their father would miss them terribly, he would not miss the problems they brought upon him. He wasn't comforted at all when the third son promised to write. That son never told the truth.

"Where do you think we should go?" asked the first brother.

"I think our only choice is to go to the big city. If we fight, steal and lie there, perhaps nobody will even notice us. After all, everyone does that in the big city," said the second brother.

"I agree," replied the third brother, but the brothers didn't know if they could believe him.

The three brothers walked on in the direction of the big city. They didn't know it at the time, but people in the city faced a serious problem. Guarding the road into the city was a genie, and he wasn't the friendly kind that granted wishes. This was an evil genie. He frequently beat, robbed and even killed anyone he found on the roads around the city once the sun went down. Of course, it was a terrible situation for everyone who lived in the city and even worse for guests who didn't know anything about it until it was too late.

Fortunately for the brothers, they arrived safely in the city late in the afternoon. Unfortunately, they didn't blend into the city as well as they had hoped. While two of the brothers searched for a place to stay for the night, the first brother decided to explore the city. He was puzzled when he saw stores closing up earlier than he expected. The reason was simple. Nobody wanted to be out after dark and risk meeting the genie. Unfortunately, the brother knew nothing about that. He watched as families rushed into their homes and heard them locking their doors behind them. But, most interesting of all, he watched the mayor of the city leave the bank with what had to be a bag full of gold.

"What's going on with this bag of gold?" he thought.

Never afraid of a little trouble or mischief, the brother followed the man to his house. It was simply too irresistible not to. The mayor didn't even have time to put his gold away before the first brother knocked on his door.

"Who would ever come out this late in the day when the genie will soon be on the prowl? There must be something terrible happening in the city!" thought the mayor. He left the bag of gold on his table and rushed to his front door to see what was the matter.

"Hello, I am new in town," announced the brother. "In fact, I just arrived today. I knew you would want to greet me with kola nut since you are the mayor. That's why I have come to meet you."

"Won't you please come in," offered the mayor. "It's a little unusual to have a guest so late in the day, but I can always share kola nut with a new friend." He quickly hurried into the kitchen to get some. However, the moment the mayor left the room, the brother snatched the bag of gold and was out the door.

"Where did you say you were from?" asked the mayor as he returned to an empty living room. Hmmm . . . that's so very strange." And then, he noticed that the bag of gold was missing from the table. Even though the sun was setting, he ran into the street screaming, "Rogue! Rogue! Did anyone see where that young man went? He's stolen a bag of gold from my home!"

It didn't take long at all for his neighbors to come to his rescue. At the mention of gold, the entire neighborhood ran into the streets searching for that rogue. It was quite a large commotion that just never happened at that time of day.

"There he is!" cried an old woman. "I just saw him dash around the corner."

The neighbors raced after the thief. The two other brothers, about to settle into their new room, also heard the noise outside. "I think that must have something to do with our brother. He always finds trouble and needs me to rescue him," said the second brother. "I think we had better find him."

"It didn't take very long for him to find trouble," said the third brother. This time, it certainly wasn't a lie.

When the brothers went outside, they had no trouble locating their older brother. He raced down the street towards them with an angry mob close at his heels. There were simply too many people for the second brother to fight, so the two brothers joined their brother in search of the quickest way out of the city.

The crowd chased close behind them. Well, they stayed close by until the three brothers reached the city limits. No one from the city was brave enough to leave the safety of the city when it was almost evening. That genie was just too terrible. But, again, the brothers knew nothing about the genie. Yes, they were puzzled - but they were even more relieved because the angry crowd had gotten much too close for comfort.

"What a day we've had!" cried the second brother. "First, we get kicked out of our own village, and now we are chased from the city."

"By the way, why were we chased from the city?" asked the third brother. "What did you do?"

"I sort of helped myself to a welcoming present from the mayor," confessed the first brother. "He had a bag of gold and I kind of considered it a gift."

"I don't suppose you had his permission?" asked the second brother.

"I never concern myself with details like that."

"And I will help myself to that little detail right now," growled a voice from behind them.

IT WAS THE EVIL GENIE!

"Whoever you are, you don't scare us," lied the third brother.

"I've killed much bigger men than you," replied the genie. "Didn't anyone tell you that I guarded this city? No one comes out here after dark because they fear me too much. That is why the people stopped at the city limits. You three were foolish enough to come out here, and now you will pay for it with your lives!"

"Step aside, brothers," said the second brother. "This looks like it's a job for me. I am, after all, the fighter in this family. No evil genie is a match for me."

And, he was right.

It came as quite a surprise to the genie when the second brother charged into the fight. And, to the even greater surprise of the genie, the match wasn't even close. The brother overpowered the genie as nobody had ever done before. When the fight was over and the genie was killed, the second brother cut off his head.

"What incredible luck for us!" cried the third brother as he grabbed the genie's head and placed it in a bag. "Certainly, this is our lucky day. Now we do not need to leave this city. I have a plan that will solve all our problems and hopefully take care of us for a long time to come."

"A plan?" asked his brothers.

"Yes, we will go back to the mayor tomorrow, and he will gladly welcome us. Just let me do all of the talking."

The two other brothers were not at all sure that they could trust their brother this time. But they both hoped he was telling them the truth.

In the morning, there was quite a stir throughout the city when the brothers marched back into the center of the town. The mayor cried, "Have these men taken to prison! Call for the judge! There will be no rogues allowed in our city!"

"Mayor," said the third brother, "is this how you treat the three men who have rescued your city?"

"What do you mean you have rescued us? You have personally stolen my gold and caused a riot in my city!"

"I mean to tell you, my good mayor, that we have eliminated the genie that has plagued your city for so long. It was a plan that my brothers and I devised," lied the third brother. "We had to steal the gold, so the genie would definitely want to stop us. We needed each of you last night to chase us because it attracted the genie's attention. When he saw the angry mob, he certainly had no idea he was about to fall into a deadly trap. He had no idea my second brother was such a powerful fighter."

"This is ridiculous!" cried the mayor. "If anyone could kill the genie, I would give him half of the city and its riches."

The brothers tried not to smile.

The mayor continued, "It would be the greatest day in the history of our community. We would have feasting and celebrating. You and your brothers, however, are hardly the ones to save us. You only deserve our prison, and the darkest corner of it as well. And, that is where you will go now. Guards! Arrest these rogues!"

The third brother decided it was time to open up his bag of tricks and pull out the genie's head. He'd heard enough from the mayor to know that he and his brothers would be able to stay in the town and become quite wealthy. And so, he let the genie out of the bag . . . or at least his head.

Everyone, including the mayor, gasped in disbelief.

The people in the town were simply amazed that these three brothers had rescued them from the genie. It was so unexpected! A celebration broke out and, instead of being taken to prison, the brothers were escorted to the mayor's home for a feast.

The brothers settled down in the city and became leaders in the community. They lived well and were liked by all who knew them, even if they still occasionally would fight, steal and lie.

TURTLE'S MAGIC ROCK

One day as Turtle walked down the path not far from the village, he discovered a truly unusual sight. It was a small rock that actually had a face. Turtle had never seen anything like it before. He picked up the rock for a closer look. "You have a face, my little rock," declared Turtle. "I wish you could talk to me."

There was no way for Turtle to know it at the time, but he was holding a magic rock. Whenever people asked this stone to speak, instead of talking, the rock would beat them. Smack! Crack! Attack! Every time. And since Turtle asked the rock to talk, you know what the stone did. It attacked him. Fortunately for Turtle, his trusty shell protected him from the beating.

"Hmmm . . . There must be a way for me to use this special rock," thought Turtle as soon as the attack stopped. "Maybe, possibly, it can do my hunting for me?"

It didn't take long for an idea to form in Turtle's mind.

Later in the day, he saw Black Deer getting a drink down by the stream. "My friend, I have found something very unusual to share with you. I'd like you to see this magic rock. It has a face, and I think it will talk to you if you speak to it," said Turtle.

"A talking rock, you say?" asked Black Deer. "I have never heard of anything like that. I must see this."

Turtle directed Black Deer back down the path to the rock. It was in a remote part of the bush, but that was all a part of the turtle's plan.

Turtle picked up the rock and showed it to Black Deer. "Go ahead and ask it to talk," the turtle urged.

"I feel really silly right now. Are you sure about this?" asked Black Deer.

"Trust me. What is there to lose in trying?"

"Okay," said Black Deer. He looked at the rock and said, "I want you to talk to me."

Of course, the rock didn't talk. Smack! Crack! Attack! Instead, it lunged for the deer and killed him right there on the spot.

Turtle slowly dragged the body home. His family had good meat in their soup that night. It was quite a celebration for the turtle clan. As you might guess, someone as slow as Turtle rarely ever caught any food.

Turtle's plan was very successful. As time passed, he lured Monkey, Leopard and even Elephant to his magic rock. The elephant provided enough meat to last a long time, a very long time. There was no such thing as a hunger season as long as Turtle had his magic rock and kept his very special secret.

Eventually, Anteater, Red Deer and Hippo also were lured to the rock. The results were always the same. Smack! Crack! Attack! And then, Turtle dragged the animals back to his home. This way of hunting was better than anything Turtle had ever imagined. He was so thankful for this lucky rock.

One day Turtle saw Spider resting on his web. "There isn't a lot of meat on Spider's bones," he thought, "but a meal is a meal." So, Turtle called to the spider and said, "Come and see the unusual rock I have found. It's actually a magic rock. It has a face and will even talk to you if you ask it to."

"Humph! What kind of nonsense are you talking about, Turtle? I don't believe in talking rocks," replied Spider.

"Well, if you don't believe me, you can just ask Leopard, Bush Hog, Anteater or Elephant," said Turtle. "Every one of them has come and seen my rock."

Suddenly, Spider was a lot more interested in that rock. Turtle had given him more information than he realized. Spider knew that all of those animals, as well as several more, were missing from their jungle community. He wondered, "Could this so-called magic rock have anything to do with their disappearances?" Spider decided that he needed to go with Turtle to investigate this rock, but he also knew that he had to be extremely careful.

Turtle guided Spider into the bush and down the path to the secluded spot where he hid the magic stone. When Turtle pointed out the special rock, the careful Spider said nothing.

"Well?" asked Turtle.
"Well, what?"
"Well, aren't you going to ask the rock to talk?"
"I'm really not sure if I believe in talking rocks."
"You can trust me, Spider. I've heard the rock talk several times."
"Well, I don't really know what to say to a rock," admitted Spider.
"Just ask him."
"Ask the rock what?" replied the careful Spider.

Turtle was not known for his patience. At this point, he cried out, "You're supposed to say, 'Rock, will you speak to me?'"

The words came out of his mouth before Turtle even realized what he had said. Smack! Crack! Attack! This time the rock's aim was true to its mark. It lunged at the turtle and struck the back of his head.

It killed him instantly.
Spider smiled to himself. The mystery was solved. But, he still had to be careful. He decided not to ask the rock if it would help him bury the turtle.

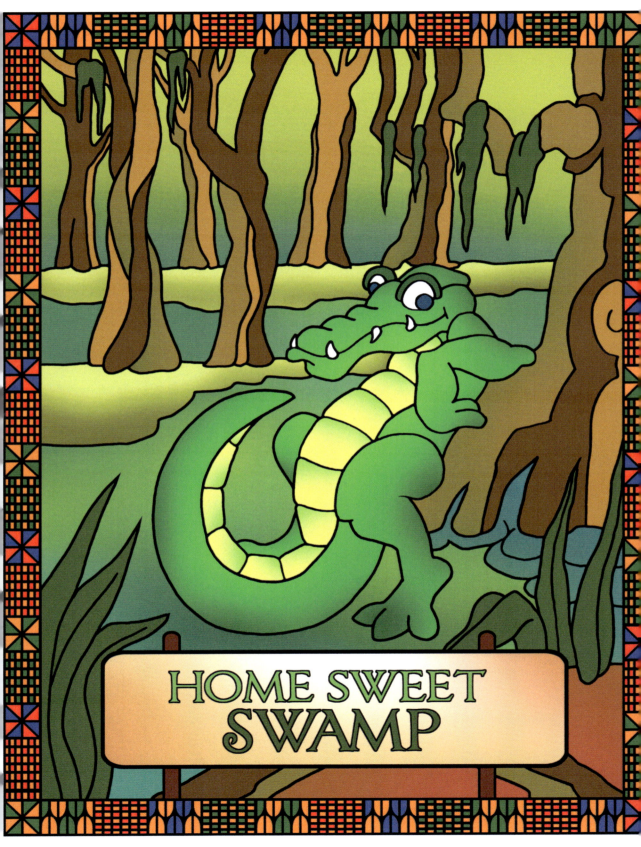

CHAPTER 3

BEAUTY IS ONLY SKIN DEEP

"Father, please send this man away from here. You know that I cannot marry him," cried the beautiful daughter. "He is simply too tall for me."

"Yes, my daughter, I will send the young man away," replied her father. "But what about this other fine young man? Could he be the one you have been waiting for?"

"Oh, no, Father! He's much too short for me. Send him away with the other one."

Every day it was the same story. Always. Young men came hoping to meet the beautiful daughter, win her hand in marriage and live happily ever after. She turned them all away. And, she had her reasons. They were always too big or too small, too wise or too foolish, too old or too young, too strong or too weak. It seemed that no one would satisfy the young girl. Nobody was just right in her eyes. And still, more and more young men arrived, hoping that they might be the one to win the love of this beautiful young woman.

Even deep in the bush, along a river where men seldom ever traveled, Crocodile heard about her beauty. "I must see this fair maiden for myself," he thought. "If she is as lovely as they say, I will certainly marry her."

Crocodile was nobody's fool. He realized that green was probably not the girl's favorite skin color. But, the clever reptile knew what to do. He took some country medicine that for a while would change him into a human being. Yes, it was powerful medicine and it indeed changed him into a very handsome young man. The medicine didn't, however, give him any clothes. As he left the river and headed in the direction of the city where the lovely girl lived, the man found it necessary to borrow things along the way.

In the first village that Crocodile, er . . . the young man came to, he found a person on the other side of a fence. "My friend, could you please lend me some pants? I want to go to the city and marry a beautiful girl."

"How did you end up with no pants? " asked the villager.

"It's a complicated story and I don't have time to tell you if I am to marry this bride."

"Okay, my friend, I think I have some pants that will fit you."

In the next village, the man found it much easier to borrow a shirt. As it turned out, the closer he came to the city, the more the man was able to borrow. No one could refuse such a handsome young man. By the time he reached the city, he also had a tie, a straw hat, new shoes, a gold watch and a walking stick.

The young man looked like quite the handsome gentleman when he strolled into the city. Everyone wanted to know who this new stranger could be. When the beautiful daughter saw him from a distance, she informed her father that he was the one that she was going to marry. Her mind was made up.

"But you've never even talked to him," argued the father. "How can you know what kind of person he is?"

"Father, if you don't go meet this man and make the arrangements, then I will go and do it personally," warned the daughter. "This is the one I choose."

The father had no choice. His daughter had made up her mind, and he knew how stubborn she was. So, he made all of the necessary arrangements. In a few days, a big wedding celebration took place. There was plenty of music, dancing and food. The feasting went on for days. No one could ever remember seeing a more beautiful couple.

After the wedding, plans were made for the newlyweds to move back to the man's home. He never told them he lived in a swamp by a big river. He simply said he lived deep in the bush at the end of the path. All of the bride's friends decided to help her move her belongings. Together they followed the path into the bush.

The bride and her friends were so busy laughing and talking that nobody noticed they had left the husband a small distance behind. He walked alone with his own thoughts. He felt the country medicine wearing off. When he returned the walking stick, he noticed his fingernails had grown longer. When he returned the watch, he saw that his skin had turned slightly green. The shoes were hard to remove by the time he returned them because his feet had grown so big.

The girls continued on the path never noticing the husband. They all knew to follow the path until it completely ended. It was an easy path to follow. The husband carried the hat to its owner because it no longer fit on his head. When he returned the tie, it almost wouldn't go around his massive neck.

As he reached the village where he borrowed the shirt, the owner ran away in fear. "What happened to that nice young man?" he cried. "Was he eaten by a crocodile?" The villager didn't wait around for an answer.

By the time the groom returned his pants, all of the country medicine had worn off. He was fully and completely a crocodile once again. The man on the other side of the fence stayed behind it for his safety.

But the bride and her friends never noticed any of these changes to the groom. The girls only stopped their laughing when they finally reached the end of the path.

"Where is the small village?" one of the girls asked.

"I have no idea," replied the bride.

"And where is the fine house?" they all wondered.

"All I see is a river and a swamp," said the puzzled bride.

The crocodile cleared his throat and declared, "This is my home. My bride and I welcome you."

The girls recognized his voice, but when they turned around, they did not see the handsome young man. They saw a huge, green crocodile.

The girls fled in fear leaving their beautiful friend frozen in terror.

The new bride knew that she had made a terrible mistake. She also knew that there was no way to escape her fate. The crocodile pulled his lovely bride into the swamp to show her their new home.

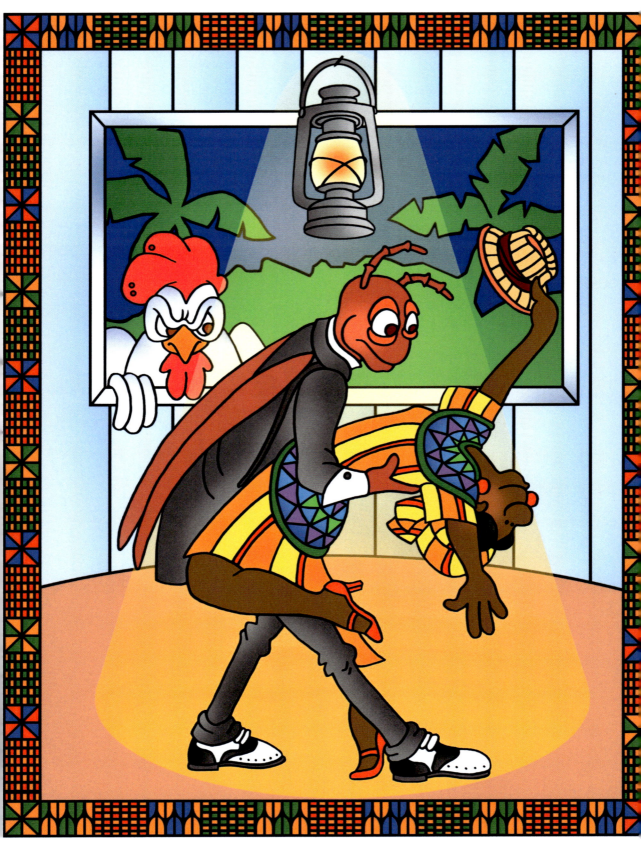

COCKROACH AND ROOSTER

Cockroach and Rooster lived together in a village deep in the bush. They did everything together. They went to the market together. They swam together. If Rooster prepared cassava leaves, Cockroach was at his side. If Cockroach hunted in the bush, Rooster walked along with him. It didn't surprise anyone when they decided to make a farm together.

The woman who lived next door to them shook her head and warned them. "It's one thing to play together all the time, but when you do serious work together, it can really test your friendship. I predict that this will come to no good."

"Silly woman," crowed Rooster, "nothing will come between us."

"Go find something worth gossiping about," said Cockroach. "This is nonsense."

"Humph! You mark my words!" warned the old woman. "I know what I'm talking about."

"Humph!" replied Rooster. "One thing is certain. That old woman knows how to talk."

The two friends decided on a plot and began their preparations. They worked the first day very seriously clearing the land. On their way home, they were too tired to pay attention to the old woman laughing at them.

On the second day, Cockroach had about all the work he could stand. He was lazy and quickly realized that working on a farm was not for him. Besides, he had to find a way to get out of work that day and get to Cow's party that afternoon. When the two friends stopped for lunch, Cockroach told his friend a lie. "Rooster, I'm not feeling well. I think I must go to the clinic this afternoon."

"If you are not well, by all means, go see the doctor," said Rooster. "I'll continue here for a while. You go see the doctor and get some rest. I'll fix supper tonight. The only thing that you should do is take care of yourself."

Getting rest was the farthest thing from Cockroach's mind. With the big party at Cow's place beginning late in the afternoon, Cockroach needed time to get ready for the celebration. He washed and pressed his best suit and topped it off with a fine straw hat. When preparations were finished, he waited impatiently for the hours to pass.

As Cockroach stepped out of the house to go to the party, the old woman shrieked with laughter. "I've never seen anyone work on the farm dressed like that! Nobody dresses like that to go to the doctor, either!"

Cockroach tried to ignore her as he continued on his way to the party. He heard the old woman laughing for a long time.

Meanwhile, back at the farm, Rooster worked doubly hard. He tried to do his friend's share of the work as well. "If Cockroach is so sick," thought Rooster, "I don't want him to worry about unfinished work. He needs his rest, so I'll do just a little bit extra for him."

It was well after dark before Rooster trudged home, exhausted. However, as he neared the village, he quickened his steps. He wanted to see how Cockroach felt. Rooster quietly crept into his friend's bedroom so he would not disturb him, but Cockroach wasn't there. He quickly searched the kitchen, the living room and the back porch. Cockroach was nowhere to be found, and the rooster was very concerned. "Was my friend so sick he had to go to the hospital?" he wondered.

As Rooster came around the yard to the front porch, he heard the old neighbor woman call, "Are you looking for that cockroach? Is that what you're doing?"

"Yes," replied Rooster, "he was very sick this afternoon and had to leave the farm. I'm afraid something might be terribly wrong."

"Ha! The only thing terribly wrong is the way that lazy cockroach is treating his best friend," snapped the old woman.

"What do you mean?"

"Your friend wasn't sick at all. He didn't rest. He saw no doctor. Instead, he spent the entire afternoon preparing for the big party going on at Cow's place."

"HE DID WHAT?" crowed Rooster.

"You heard me," replied the woman. "That's where he is this very moment. If you don't believe me, then go see for yourself."

That's exactly what Rooster did.

He didn't clean up. He didn't change into his best clothes. Rooster didn't care if his comb was shiny or his claws were cleaned. He simply rushed to Cow's party as fast as his legs could take him.

Now Cockroach had the time of his life at the party. He was such a fine dancer that all of the ladies wanted their turn with him. He was so busy dancing that he almost didn't see Rooster leap for him.

Chairs flew in all directions, tables of food were overturned and the party turned into a mass of confusion as Rooster chased after that cockroach.

"I trusted you! I worked all day doing your job as well as mine," cried Rooster. "How can you treat me like this?"

"Let me explain," cried Cockroach.

"There is nothing to explain," replied Rooster. "While I was planting our farm, you were here eating and dancing. Well, I'm about to have my dessert, and you look very juicy!"

Cockroach barely escaped out the window without Rooster snapping off part of his leg. By the time Rooster ran out the front door, Cockroach had hidden himself deep in the bush. The friendship and the party were over. There was no way of repairing their bond. To this day, when Rooster sees Cockroach, he chases him off into the bush. And, whenever the old woman sees this, she just laughs.

A RACE TO REMEMBER

There were many activities scheduled in the village to celebrate the big feast. The chief gave introductions to honored guests from near and far. Cultural dancers performed traditional dances to the sound of the drum beat. However, what most people remember from the day was the race between Turtle and Rabbit.

The story really began a few weeks before the feast when Turtle and Rabbit sat around one hot afternoon playing checkers under the shade of a plum tree. Rabbit had a habit of bragging about his speed and this day was no exception.

"Turtle, my friend, I am so fast and so graceful whenever I race. I truly wish that I could just watch myself run. It must be beautiful, such a magnificent sight to see."

"Oh, brother," mumbled Turtle. "It's your turn. Just move another checker."

"Honestly," asked Rabbit, "have you ever seen anything as elegant as my running?"

"Honestly, I've never seen anything or heard anyone as conceited as you!"

"Is that so? You're just jealous because I'm so quick and you're so absolutely slow!"

"Jealous? Slow!" snapped the turtle. "Don't humor yourself. I could beat you in a race and even have time for a nap halfway through the contest!"

"Ha! Is that what you really think?" replied Rabbit. "There is a race at the big feast for a bag of rice. I'll shame you that day and take home the rice."

"That's what you think!" scoffed Turtle. "You are so wrong, so completely wrong! When the race is finished, you are invited to my house for rice."

"No way!" cried Rabbit. "When the race is finished, you come to eat at my house. But, I'm not sure you'll like what my wife is going to make. We'll be having TURTLE SOUP!"

Obviously, the checker game ended right then. Turtle threw the board in Rabbit's face and stormed away. Well, as fast as a turtle can storm away. Neither animal spoke to - or even looked at - the other as the weeks passed and the big feast approached. Rabbit was seen running laps around the village each day while Turtle walked from house to house of each turtle in the community.

By the time the feast day arrived, everyone knew about the race and could talk of little else. The race began at noon, and even the chief and honored guests pushed in the crowd to get the very best view of the contest. The only one obviously not present when the race began was Rabbit's wife. She was home putting a pot of water on the fire to prepare for the bag of rice her husband planned to bring home.

Suddenly, the whistle blew, and the race started!

Rabbit teased, "See you at my house for soup."

He darted off into the bush leaving Turtle in his dust. After fifty yards or so, as Rabbit looked back to check on his competition, he nearly tripped over the turtle right there at his feet.

"What's the matter, Rabbit? Do you think the only way to beat me is to step on me?"

Rabbit was too surprised to speak. He couldn't believe that Turtle was actually there and ahead of him. Rabbit raced on past him deeper into the bush. However, fifty yards later, there was Turtle again.

"Hi. What kept you? Are you going to be late for dinner at my house, too?" asked Turtle with a grin.

Rabbit raced on deeper into the bush. It happened again and again. About every fifty yards, Rabbit ran into a clearing and saw Turtle there waiting for him to catch up. Halfway through the race, Rabbit's confidence was nearly shattered when he came upon Turtle obviously just getting up from a nap.

"Excuse me," yawned Turtle. "I was just so sleepy waiting for you. Let's continue the race."

Rabbit ran into the bush with tears of frustration in his eyes. Again, and again, he met Turtle on the path. And then, in the distance, he heard what he thought sounded like thunder. But as he left the bush, Rabbit realized it was not thundering that he heard but rather cheering from the crowd. As he ran closer to the village, he saw Turtle cross the finish line and stand there waving. "Come join me, Rabbit!" he cried. "There's plenty of room for you with me at the finish line."

The embarrassed Rabbit ran to the finish line but didn't stop. He continued on to his home. It was the only place he could go to hide his shame. And, he had a lot of that to hide!

Turtle, on the other hand, celebrated the moment with the crowd before joyously carrying the bag of rice home. The entire turtle community came over for a victory feast. Every turtle had worked hard for this moment. Turtle and his friends knew that he could never beat Rabbit in a race unless they tricked him. And, they had all decided it was time to teach Rabbit a lesson. Since all turtles looked alike to Rabbit, Turtle stationed his friends and family every fifty yards of the way along the race's path. Rabbit never realized that each turtle he passed during the race was part of a large circle of family and friends. That was a secret for the turtle community. Keeping that secret somehow made the rice taste so much sweeter.

BREAD FOR AN OLD BEGGAR

Many years ago, in a village, there lived an old beggar who was not able to take care of himself. He continually went to different houses in the village for his needs. He was a kindly old man that few people could ever turn away. In the same village, there was a certain rich man who always had some extra coins or food when the beggar passed by his gate. Frequently, the rich man would invite the old beggar into his home to eat. The rich man's children adored the beggar. While most adults rarely had time for children, the beggar was always happy to play games or tell stories to the children. Unfortunately, the rich man's wife was not like the rest of her family. She disliked the old beggar. "That beggar is an embarrassment to me," complained the wife. "He dresses poorly and smells bad. I do not like him in our house."

"It is not good to feel this way about the old man," replied the rich husband. "We do not know what the future holds for us. Perhaps someday we will also need to beg."

But the woman's resentment grew. She could not be as generous as her husband. She only wanted that poor old beggar removed from her presence. If her husband would not do anything about the problem, then she would have to find her own solution.

One day as she baked bread, an idea came to the woman. It was so clever that she knew it would end her embarrassment with that old beggar once and for all. She decided she would bake two loaves of bread, especially for the old man. However, they would not be ordinary loaves. These loaves would be baked with a very strong poison included in the recipe. She determined to find a poison that had no possible cure.

Later that day as the old beggar passed by the rich man's gate, the rich wife saw him. "I have made these fresh loaves of bread especially for you," she said with a wicked smile. "They are still warm so you will want to eat them right away."

The beggar was very surprised by the woman's kindness. He would not refuse such a generous offer. However, he had just eaten and wasn't hungry at that moment. He thanked the woman, put the loaves in his pocket and continued down the road. The woman smiled as she returned into her home. Her problems would soon be over.

ONCE UPON WEST AFRICA

Further on down the road, the old beggar was pleasantly attacked by the rich man's children on their way home from school. "Oh!" squealed one daughter, "we're so happy to see you. Will you tell us a story?"

"Please come back to the house to play games with us," begged the youngest son.

"I'm hungry," pouted the smallest girl. "Do you have anything to eat?"

"Children, children," laughed the old beggar. "You ask so many questions. Yes, I have a story to tell you. Yes, I'll play a game. However, I must first run an errand before I can come to your home. And finally, I do have some food. Your mother just gave me some fresh bread. You may eat it. I'm not really hungry."

The children gobbled down the bread and merrily continued on their way home. By the time they reached their mother, instead of their usual cheerful smiles, they greeted her with complaints of stomach aches.

"Did you eat any sweets to upset your stomach?" asked their mother as she gently hugged them.

"No, Mother, we only ate the bread you gave to the old beggar man."

A terror seized the mother's heart as she fled the room in tears. The evil she had planned for someone else had come back to her family, and there was nothing she could do to stop it.

What? Seriously? No! The story can't end that way. Okay, I get it. The nasty woman should learn a lesson. But, there has to be another way for her to learn it.

Fortunately, there is.

Go back a few paragraphs and check out a different ending.

Further on down the road, the old beggar was pleasantly attacked by the rich man's children on their way home from school. "Oh!" squealed one daughter, "we're so happy to see you. Will you tell us a story?"

"Please come back to the house to play games with us," begged the youngest son.

The old beggar laughed. "You always make me feel so welcome. Yes, I have a story to tell you. Yes, I'll play a game. However, I must first run an errand before I can come to your home. And, by the way, I just came from your place. Your mother gave me some fresh bread, but I'm not really hungry. Here, take it."

"We'll take it," replied the oldest son, "but we are not hungry right now. We saw Papa by the marketplace and he bought us some candy."

"Don't tell Mama," squealed one of the daughters.

"Your secret is safe with me," the old beggar promised.

The children scattered as they merrily headed for home. The old beggar continued on his errand. When the children reached home, the oldest son added the bread to the other loaves his mother baked that day. Then, all of the children went out to play.

Nobody was in the house when the woman grabbed a loaf for her afternoon snack.

CAT KNOWS HIS LOVE HAS ITS LIMITS

The beauty of the young rat was known far and wide throughout the land. Many handsome chiefs and rich young men attempted to win her love. They all failed. She turned each of them away. Still, every week another young man arrived in the village, hoping he would be the one to win her heart.

Young Cat did not have to travel far to see the lovely rat. He grew up with her in the same village. In fact, they were next-door neighbors. Their families had become close friends over the years. Young Cat had secretly been in love with his beautiful neighbor for most of his life. When he decided that he too would ask to marry the young rat, the two families were so very happy. Secretly their mothers had hoped for this arrangement ever since either of them could remember. It was the best news they could have hoped for.

Everyone in the village was happy about the possible marriage - everyone, that is, except for the lovely young rat.

"Oh, Mother, what should I do?" wailed the little rat. "He is such a fine cat - and he would certainly make an excellent husband - except I cannot marry him."

"But why, my dear?" asked her distraught mother. "Why can't you marry him?"

"He is a cat," explained the daughter, "and all cats have such very long noses. You know it's true. I cannot possibly marry anyone with such a nose."

The young cat truly loved the beautiful rat. "There is nothing I would not do for her," he declared. "There is no wish I could ever deny her." When he learned that the rat would marry him if his nose were not so long, the cat set about trying to find a way to shorten his nose. This problem had to have a solution.

He asked the women around the market, "Do you have something to make my nose shorter? Is there a special herb or powder that can help me with this?"

"We have plenty of peppers, grated cassava, all kinds of greens, ripe plums and even bug-a-bugs," they replied, "but there is nothing in the market to make a nose shorter.

"Doctor," begged the young cat, "I need your help and I need it right now. Is there some kind of medicine that you have to make my nose shorter?"

"I'm sorry," apologized the doctor. "I can stop a runny nose or remove a wart from the nose, but there is nothing I can do to make your nose shorter."

"Isn't there anybody who can help me shorten my nose?" cried the helpless cat.

"I can shorten your nose," said the village blacksmith. "It isn't a difficult thing for me to do. If you come by my shop, we can do it this afternoon."

"You're my hero today," replied the cat. "Be sure to save the date for my wedding. You'll be a guest of honor!"

Naturally, the cat went to the blacksmith's shop that afternoon. Absolutely nothing could have kept him away. The blacksmith heated his knife over the hot coals. "It's going to hurt a little," he warned, "but it will not take long at all."

"It'll be worth the pain when I get to marry my little rat," said Cat. He was certain. With his new short nose, nothing could stop the wedding he'd always dreamed about.

And then, the blacksmith quickly snipped off the cat's nose.

The doctor bandaged Cat's face and sent him home to recover for a few weeks.

Now nobody told the blacksmith how much of Cat's nose to remove. And, there are times when you need to be very clear about giving instructions. This was one of those times. When the bandages came off, and the nose was healed, Cat hardly had a nose at all. The blacksmith had certainly shortened his nose.

The young cat looked in the mirror and beamed. "It's all healed up and I'm ready to show it to my lovely rat."

"It may take some getting used to," replied his mother.

"Oh, no," said Cat. "It's exactly what she asked for. And, I'd gladly do anything for her."

Cat raced over to the rats' home to show off his new and shortened nose.

"Look! My darling, look! My nose is all healed now. Isn't it lovely? It's just what you wanted!"

"Oh, no," gasped the young rat.

"Huh? No?"

"What happened? Where is your nose?"

"But this is what you asked for . . ."

"You have no nose at all! I can't possibly marry someone with no nose," cried the lovely rat. "This has all been a terrible mistake. I'm so very sorry."

This was too much for the young cat!

"What do you mean?" spat the cat. "First, my nose was too long, and now it is too short! There is just no pleasing you." Enraged with the whole situation, he chased the little rat out of the room, destroying half of the furniture in the process. The rat raced off the porch and from her yard. Cat trailed closely behind. "If I ever catch you," he cried, "I'll pound you in the mortar and see what that does to your nose."

Rat knew he meant exactly what he said. Fortunately for her, she narrowly escaped his claws. The wedding was off, the friendship was forever broken and to this day, Cat "nose" he was terribly wronged by a very lovely rat.

EVERYONE IS NOT HAPPY WITH EVERYONE

"I should have made better plans," muttered Turtle. "It takes four days to walk to the paramount chief's home, and his feast is tomorrow. Why did I put things off so late? Now, how am I going to get to the celebration?"

Most of the other animals had already left for the party. Only the birds remained in the area. They could easily fly to the celebration and would not be late. In order to attend the feast, Turtle knew he would need the help of the birds. Trying to look as sick as possible, he crawled to their nest. "Could you please help me? I haven't felt well these past few days," lied Turtle. "It has kept me from leaving earlier for the paramount chief's feast. Is there any way you can help carry me there tomorrow?"

"That is not happening, Turtle," replied Bird. "We don't take passengers."

"My dear, just look at him. Turtle has been sick. I think we should help him," whispered his wife. "It wouldn't hurt to take a passenger this one time."

"Okay, maybe this one time," agreed Bird. "Turtle, we'll take you this once. Come to our nest in the morning with a strong stick about your height."

Turtle crawled away with a hidden smile. It was easier than he expected. Finding one strong stick was certainly a lot better than walking for four days. "Those two birds might think I'm sick," Turtle said to himself, "but I don't know when I've ever felt better."

In the morning, Turtle returned to the birds with the stick they requested. The plan was simple. Turtle bit down hard in the middle while the birds grabbed on to each end of the stick with their feet. With no effort at all, they lifted Turtle into the air as they flew on to the paramount chief's celebration. Once - only once - Turtle looked down and almost screamed. He somehow held the scream deep inside because he knew what would happen if he ever opened his mouth for any reason. Turtle had never been so high before in his life. He found the travel easier if he just kept his eyes closed.

The ride didn't take long. Soon they were at the feast. Once Turtle was on solid ground, he even enjoyed the idea of flight. Everyone was in a party mood.

"The chief's wife has asked us to make up special names for ourselves," said Antelope. "I think 'Long Horns' will be my name for the party."

"You can call me 'Tusks,'" giggled the Elephant. "And, Lion over there wants to be called 'Royal' for the day."

The birds decided "Yellow Feathers" would work as their party names. And last of all, it was Turtle who named himself. "Please call me 'Everyone' during the celebration," he requested.

"Everyone?" asked Mrs. Bird.

"Yes, that's my request."

"Very good," said the chief's wife. "Now that we have our names, let the party begin. I think the food is now ready. Everyone, it's time to eat."

"That's my name and that's what I have been waiting for," replied Turtle with a smile. "I guess I'm the only one to eat now. She did say, 'Everyone, it's time to eat.' "

The other animals were not at all pleased with Turtle's name. Many were hungry after having walked for days, and now Turtle was eating all of the food. However, Turtle didn't let this concern him. There was too much delicious food to enjoy, so he wasn't worried about what the others thought of him or his name.

The paramount chief was vexed, and his wife was as well. Turtle had ruined her party.

"Who invited him?" growled the chief.

"We invited everyone," she replied.

That made Turtle smile.

"We are not using that name any more during this party," declared the chief.

Several of the hungrier animals left the feast to find food elsewhere. Those who remained were no longer cheerful. The party mood ended as they watched Turtle finish up one dish after another.

And then, he burped!

"Thank you so very much for an extremely wonderful meal," declared Turtle. "The palm butter was especially good, and 'Everyone' loved the jollof rice."

"How can you make fun of me after treating me like this?" cried the chief's wife. "Go away from here. Leave my party! Trust me, you will never be invited back to my home."

Bird was not pleased with Turtle either and wanted to leave without him. There was simply no way he wanted to carry Turtle home.

"But, Bird," reminded his wife, "we promised to carry him. Just because he acted poorly is no reason for us to act the same. I, for one, do not want to go back on my word."

"I suppose you're right," muttered Bird. "But I'm really not happy that you are right this time."

A much heavier Turtle once again bit on to the stick, and the birds carried him high into the sky. Just before they were out of sight, the paramount chief called out, "Good-bye! Everyone can now have a good time now that 'Everyone' has left our party!"

Turtle opened his mouth to say, "I believe that 'Everyone' already had a good time," but the words never came out. As soon as he opened his mouth, his grip on the stick loosened. He fell from the clouds and crashed on the ground shattering his shell into many small pieces.

True to their word, the birds came to his rescue. They carried Turtle to his home and patched his shell back together. Today his shell is still covered with patches. Turtle is continually reminded that everyone should treat everyone in the same way that everyone would want everyone to treat themselves.

HOME SWEET BOA'S HOME

"When is this rainy season ever going to end?" complained the old boa constrictor to himself. "It makes everything in my life so much more difficult. It is hard to find food, and there's never a warm, dry place for me to snuggle up and sleep. I'm just too miserable to put up with this much longer."

The old snake lived in a big tree on the top of a hill which no longer provided much protection from the rain. Boa didn't want to face another day, let alone another storm in that tree. As he looked upon a village down the hill, an idea formed in his mind. "Why don't I just move down to that community? There must be someone with enough room who is willing to take me into their home."

Although Boa had never actually been to the village before, he was very hopeful as he slithered down the hill. "Just please help me find a warm place to sleep," he thought. The village was rather small, and the boa was warmly greeted with kola nuts upon his arrival.

"Is there any place where I might stay here?" the boa asked. "I really just need something for the rainy season. But, if I like it, I could stay on longer."

"I know a place," cried a young boy, who then directed the snake to a large home in the center of the village.

"The woman who lives here should be able to help you," said the child.

"Thank you so very much," replied the boa. As the child scampered away to play, the boa couldn't help but consider just how delicious that little boy looked.

His thoughts were interrupted as the woman of the home came out to meet him at her front door. She was a kind woman who was well-known in the area for her fine cooking. Thick red palm butter was her specialty.

"What brings you to our little village?" she asked with a welcoming smile.

"My old tree just isn't protecting me as I need in the rains. I'm hoping to find a dry place to rest."

"I think we have just the place for you," declared the woman. "Whenever guests come to our village, they generally stay with my family and me. This house is filled with warmth and activity. You may have noticed that I have many, many children."

"I may have heard them, just a little."

"So, it's settled. Welcome to our village and my home," said the woman. "One of my children will show you to your room. Feel free to stay as long as you like."

"That is so very kind of you," replied the boa. "It will be at least until the rainy season is over."

It didn't take long for the boa to feel right at home with the family. The children enjoyed sliding on his back, and he enjoyed their laughter. As the evening approached, the boa drew closer to the fire and observed as the woman prepared the meal.

Boa was amazed as he watched the family. There was a constant flow of children running in and out of the house. "This woman has so many children," Boa wondered aloud. "They are simply everywhere I look. And, I must say, they seem to come in all shapes and sizes. Some are tall while others are small. Some are older while many are still very young. However, they all look so delicious, and here I sit so very hungry."

The snake's thoughts were distracted by a little girl who jumped back and forth over his tail.

Boa whispered, only to himself, "I think I might just swallow this juicy one. I'm sure she would help to make my body smooth and healthy. After all, I've been hungry this rainy season, and I think that little girl might be the solution to my problems."

The little girl missed her mark. Instead of jumping over the snake, she landed directly on the tip of his tail.

"That settles it," the old snake muttered. "This woman has so many children, I seriously doubt if she'll miss this one. I'm going to have a treat later in the evening when everyone is asleep. Maybe in a few days, I'll try the small boy over there too?"

Perhaps the boa was too close to the woman's cooking fire. He certainly spoke louder than he intended. He thought he was just talking to himself.

He was wrong.

The woman sampled the beans gravy as she cooked by the fire. She frowned. "If only I had some juicy, tender chunks of boa constrictor meat in this," wished the woman aloud. "Maybe a hunter with a really sharp knife will soon pass by, and we can fix my soup right away?"

Her words shocked the old boa constrictor. "How can you talk about me like that? What kind of person would welcome me into her home and then plan to eat me?"

The woman just glared at the snake.

"Don't you humans know how to welcome guests into your home properly?"

The woman stopped stirring her soup and then shook her cooking spoon in his face. She looked directly in the boa constrictor's eyes and declared, "If you do not like my words, then it is you who should be embarrassed."

"What do you mean that I should be embarrassed?" hissed the snake.

"I was only suggesting to treat you in the same way you wanted to treat me. How dare you come into my house and consider swallowing my children! What kind of guest are you?"

The woman grabbed her pestle, ready to pound something other than rice in her mortar. "Now move away from my house! Leave my village! Get out of here. You are not welcome among my people," scolded the woman. "And believe my words, if you ever return to my village, I promise you that I will locate that hunter and serve him a very delicious meal!"

The boa constrictor fled the village. He returned to his damp home in the tree on top of the hill and has never been welcomed among people ever since.

LEOPARD'S BURNING FEAR

It is a well-known fact that Leopard is a fine hunter and fears no animal in the bush. However, this wasn't always the case. Long ago when many animals used to live together in villages, there was one animal that always frightened Leopard. It may come as a surprise, but it was Rooster.

If Leopard was taking a bath when Rooster came to the stream, he ran into the bushes to hide. If Rooster appeared while Leopard was eating, he fled from his food. If Leopard spotted Rooster at the market, he immediately left, even if he had nothing to eat that day!

Everyone in the village knew about Leopard's fear of Rooster, but nobody really understood why. What was his problem? There were several rumors, but nothing could be proven. The most curious animal who wanted to understand Leopard's unusual behavior was Rooster himself.

One sunny afternoon while Rooster walked outside of the village, he came upon a small clearing in the bush where Leopard was resting. Before Leopard had a chance to escape, Rooster asked the question that was on his mind. "Leopard, I know you are a fine hunter. Most of the animals in the bush are frightened by you. Can you please tell me why you are so afraid of me? No one in the village understands this."

"To be very honest, the reason I fear you," confessed Leopard, "is because you are an animal of fire. Every time I see you, there is a flame on your head. If I ever tried to come near you, I'm sure you would burn me up."

Rooster just smiled. "Is that all? It's just my comb," crowed Rooster. "It's not fire at all. I'm sorry it has frightened you for so long. It can't burn you."

"Are you sure?" asked the doubtful leopard.

"Of course, I'm sure," replied the rooster. "If you don't believe me, you can come feel it for yourself. It won't hurt you at all."

Slowly, carefully, Leopard crept up closer to Rooster. So very uncertain he would not be burned by the comb, he cautiously reached out and touched Rooster's head. And, nothing happened! There was no fire, no burning and certainly no danger. As soon as he realized it really wasn't fire, Leopard jumped on Rooster and ate him. From that day on, Leopard feared no animal in the bush including Rooster.

PROBLEM SOLVERS AND TROUBLE MAKERS

Dog and Cat were very distressed because the chief of the town planned a grand party. But it wasn't a grand party for everyone. All of those with invitations spent days preparing for the big event, and they could talk of little else. Unfortunately, if you didn't have an invitation, there was nothing to celebrate. And, that is where Dog and Cat found themselves. They were out of luck, without an invitation, and had absolutely nothing to celebrate.

"This is not fair!" barked Dog.
"I want to go to this party!" snarled Cat.
"Me, too!"
"Who plans a party for only animals with horns?"
"I guess the chief does, but still! It's not fair!
"It certainly isn't."
"Those animals with horns are just so very proud of their invitations."
"I would be too if I had one."
"If only we had horns . . ." sighed the dog.
"Maybe there is something we can do about that," said the cat. "I have an idea that just might get us into that party."

The two friends did everything together. They farmed together, cooked together, ate together and played together. It was only natural that they would solve this problem together and attend the chief's celebration. After all, it was the social event of the season.

"Maybe we can go into the bush and find some horns somewhere?" suggested Cat.

"That just might work," her friend barked.

Dog and Cat went into the bush to hunt for an animal with horns. "If we go deep enough into the bush, you never know what can be found," said Cat. And sure enough, they found a deer that had been killed by a leopard. So, the friends had one set of horns.

"If only that leopard had been a little hungrier. If he killed two deer, we would have had two sets of horns."

"I guess we have to be thankful for what we have," said Dog.

The two friends took the horns home with them. It took some clever experimenting before they figured out how to attach them securely to their own heads. But, the puzzle was figured out well before the day of the big celebration.

"I so glad we now have these horns for the party," purred Cat with delight.

"Yes, but how do you suggest we each wear one set of horns?"

"I have that all figured out," replied Cat. "We will each share the horns and take turns attending the party."

"It's an excellent idea!"

"We can alternate our turns after two-hour shifts."

"I can certainly do a lot of dancing and dining in two hours," barked Dog.

"I think you can too," replied Cat with a smile. "When we get to the party, you can go in first."

Dog was not about to disagree with that plan.

The day of the party arrived, and all the animals with horns strutted proudly to the chief's home. Cat carefully secured the horns to Dog's head and then watched as he proudly marched to the chief's house as well. He held his head high, but his tail wagged wildly in delight.

Meanwhile, Cat waited patiently outside the house just underneath the window. She could hear everything that happened. The chief had palm wine, cane juice, palm butter, cultural dancers and lots of music. The party sounded simply wonderful.

The minutes passed by so extremely slowly for Cat. Two hours was such a very long time to sit under a window only listening. She could hardly wait for her turn.

Fortunately, on several occasions, Dog came over to the window to tell Cat what was happening. He even slipped her some of the delicious food.

"Thanks so much for the treat, my friend. Now tell me what's going on inside. I want to know everything!"

"Well, Antelope has had too much palm wine and stepped on the chief's foot as they danced."

"I wish I had seen that," cried Cat. "What else?"

"Certainly, the chief's wife is eating more than her share of the cassava leaves. But that really isn't so much of a surprise."

"I must agree with you there."

"Let me be the first to tell you that Goat cannot carry a tune to save his life."

"I wondered who that was. I couldn't figure it out, but it was simply awful."

"This is such a great party. You're going to love it when it is your turn."

Cat thought the two hours would never end. The waiting was torture. Exactly on time, Dog exited through the chief's back door and gave Cat the deer horns. When he securely fastened them on his friend's head, the cat raced into the party. She never even took the time to thank Dog for helping her put the horns on just right. Outside, under the window, Dog waited patiently for the two hours to pass and for his turn to re-enter the party.

Time passed so slowly.

To make matters even worse, Cat never brought him any food. She never came to the window to whisper about what was happening at the party. In fact, she never returned until the party completely ended. Dog was so vexed at Cat. "How could you treat me this way?" he howled. "What kind of friend would do that?"

There was really nothing that Cat could say. Her actions spoke much louder than her words. She proved she really wasn't Dog's friend at all.

THE FARMS OF TAMBA AND SAMBA

"What makes you so sure you can make a good farm?" asked Samba. "You don't even know which end of a cutlass to hold when brushing!"

"You certainly couldn't make a better farm!" snapped Tamba. "I know you too well, Samba. The only way you could get your rice to grow is to pay it."

Nobody in the village was going to get involved in the middle of this argument. They had heard these insults exchanged too many times before. Wherever these men made their farms, the villagers knew they would be far away from each other and probably in the worst possible locations for successful farms.

They were correct.

Tamba made his farm on top of a very rocky hill. His friends discussed the location among themselves, but never with Tamba. "I would have told him another spot might be better for his farm if I thought for one second that he would have listened."

"I know exactly what you mean," said another friend. "Everyone knows he never listens."

"Sadly, Tamba is just too independent for his own good," they both agreed. "He has never taken help or advice from anyone."

"And, he is proud of the fact that he can manage on his own!"

"Except, we all know that he can't."

His clothes were ragged, but Tamba would not accept any new clothes from his friends. "It's better to have old clothes than clothes that I didn't work for," he always said. "Besides, after my rice harvest, I'll have plenty of money to buy clothes."

The work at his farm was difficult since Tamba's cutlass was so old. The village blacksmith felt so bad that he made Tamba a new cutlass for free. However, when he offered it to his friend, Tamba replied, "Keep it for me. After my harvest, I will buy the cutlass. You have certainly made a very nice tool."

None of Tamba's friends were permitted to help him on his farm either. It was a very bad place for farming. The winds were strong, and the sun beat fiercely upon the hill. And to be perfectly honest, the soil was just too rocky.

It came as no surprise that Tamba's harvest was very small. When the hunger season arrived, he suffered more than most people. And still, he refused help from anyone and chose to remain in his home alone. He was not happy, but there was nothing he would allow others to do to improve the situation.

The spot along the river where Samba chose for his farm was an equally poor location. Samba selected it because he enjoyed its cool breezes. All his life, Samba had received everything he wanted. If this were the spot he wanted for his farm, nothing else would satisfy him. It didn't matter that the soil was sandy. His friends just shook their heads quietly when he said, "It is the spot I want, so it is the spot I'm going to have. Don't even try to change my mind."

Unlike Tamba, Samba was willing to accept any help he was offered. His father sent workers to make a nice home for his son along the river. Samba spent most of his days relaxing in the shade of his porch, drinking palm wine. "Why should I get my fine clothes dirty," he thought, "when my father has hired someone else to do the brushing for me?" His clothes remained nice, but the people who worked his farm did not put much effort into what they did.

Samba's tools were the best that money could buy. His father made sure of that. But even good tools need to be cared for properly. Without that care, they can quickly spoil. Unfortunately, neither Samba nor the workers bothered to care for the tools as they should have.

Samba had so much time on his hands that he grew bored. And when he was bored, he argued with his wife. It should come as no surprise that she didn't work very hard around the house. "I'm only following your example," she was heard to say on many occasions. And when she said that, there really wasn't much that Samba could say in his defense.

Everyone who knew Samba already knew that the farm was a failure even before it started. It was doomed from the start with such poor soil and Samba's unwillingness to work hard on it. The only real surprise was for Samba when his farm failed miserably. He never saw it coming. He asked his wife, "What did I do wrong? I had plenty of workers and all the right tools."

His wife wanted to suggest, "Perhaps lead by example?" She didn't say it though. It wouldn't have done any good.

His friends wanted to say, "Perhaps select a better location for your farm?" They didn't say it either. Samba would never listen to that kind of advice.

When the hunger season came, Samba had to beg for more rice from his father. He was embarrassed that his farm was such a wreck, but he never understood the problem.

The people in the village shook their heads whenever they talked about these two foolish men. "One was too proud ever to receive any help, and it made his life miserable," said an old farmer. "The other man received too much help and he, too, was unhappy."

Everyone agreed with the chief when he said, "It takes a wise man to determine when it is time to work and when it is time to accept help from friends."

THE MOTHER POT

Spider planned a feast at his home for his family and friends with plenty of rice, palm butter, cassava leaves and potato greens. The problem with all the delicious preparations was he did not have enough pots to cook all of the food. So, he went to his neighbor, Elephant, for help.

"My friend," began Spider, "I beg you, please let me use your big pot to help cook all the food for my feast."

"Of course, take the pot for the feast," replied the neighbor.

The food was prepared, and the feast began. Everyone agreed that Spider had just the right amount of food. The next morning when Spider returned the pot to Elephant, he also brought a second smaller pot.

"What's this?" asked the neighbor. "I gave you one large pot, and now you bring back my large pot and a small one."

"Your pot gave birth to a small pot while we were preparing the feast," replied Spider.

Elephant was too greedy for his own good. He knew Spider was foolish to believe a pot could give birth to another pot. It simply could not happen! However, because he was greedy, the neighbor took both pots.

A few weeks later the spider planned for another feast. Again, he needed to borrow his neighbor's pot. The greedy elephant was only too happy to lend the pot another time. He wondered, "What will that foolish spider bring to me this time?"

Again, the feast was a success. Again, there was just the right amount of food, and all the guests were pleased. However, this time Spider did not return Elephant's large pot on the following morning. All day long, the greedy neighbor waited for his pot and for whatever else the foolish spider might bring.

Spider never came that day. He never came that whole month!

Elephant waited and waited. When he could wait no longer, he thundered over to Spider's house.

"How long do I need to wait for my large pot!" he cried. "When are you going to return it?"

"I'm sorry to tell you," replied Spider, "but your pot died in childbirth."

"What!!" screamed the greedy elephant. "That's impossible! Pots cannot die! Return my pot to me immediately!"

"If pots can give birth, they can also die," answered the clever spider with a grin as he shut the door to his house in his greedy neighbor's face.

THE PALM WINE TRAP

Spider took another sip of the palm wine and mumbled to himself, "There must be something I can do to get food for my family this hunger season. We've suffered too much." He took another sip and continued to think. Suddenly, an idea came to him.

Quickly running to his home for supplies, Spider carried several items back to his palm wine tree. He brought a few chairs, a small table, cups and a large pot for boiling palm oil. His plan was now ready for action.

On the path going down to the river, Spider met Anteater. "My friend," he declared, "I haven't seen you for a long time. You must have palm wine with me this evening. The tree I have located has some especially sweet palm wine."

"I can never say no to palm wine," replied Anteater. "Just tell me where your tree is, and I'll be there this evening."

Spider went back to the tree to make sure all was ready. The last thing he did was prepare a fire to cook the palm oil in his pot. Everything was set for the anteater's arrival.

"So, here is your special tree," said Anteater as he made his way out of the bush. "Look at all of this you have here! I can't believe that you have chairs and a small table in the bush! This really must be a special place. And what are you cooking over in the pot?"

"I'm just heating some oil for the soup we'll be making later on," answered Spider.

The host quickly climbed the tree and tapped some fresh palm wine for his guest. Anteater sat back in the chair and enjoyed the evening breeze. A few moments later he had some fresh palm wine, too. Spider made sure the anteater's cup was never empty. It wasn't long before Spider had his guest quite drunk. It was exactly what he had planned.

"Oh, it's getting late. I must be going home," apologized the anteater. "But I'm afraid I've had a little too much to drink. Could you please help me get on my way? I can't seem to even see the path out of here."

"Of course, let me guide you," replied Spider. He took his guest by the hand, but did not direct him to the path home. Instead, Spider brought his guest to the pot of boiling oil and pushed him in! When the anteater was thoroughly prepared, Spider cut up the meat and took it home to his family.

Spider smiled. He had found a way to help his family through the hunger season. Over the next few weeks, Spider led several other animals to his palm wine trap in the bush. It always worked the same way. Spider always politely filled his guest's cup and managed never to drink any himself. While his trap was set, it was not a time for him to be drinking.

Throughout the bush, the animals discussed how many of their friends had mysteriously disappeared. No one had any idea what had happened. Man had not been seen or heard hunting in the area, and still, animals vanished without a trace. An uneasy feeling settled over the bush community.

For this reason, Turtle was a little suspicious when Spider invited him to drink palm wine. Turtle and Spider had never really been close friends before. Turtle wondered why suddenly he was given such a warm invitation by Spider. Still, curiosity would not permit Turtle to refuse the offer.

Turtle was very impressed when he saw the arrangements that Spider had set up in the bush. He relaxed in the chair while Spider climbed the palm tree to tap the palm wine. It wasn't long before the grinning spider returned with a large glass for his guest. Much to his surprise, Turtle refused the drink.

"What is this?" demanded Spider. "First you accept my offer to have palm wine, but now you don't drink any?"

"I will have some," explained Turtle. "It's just that in our turtle culture, the host must drink first when you are invited to have palm wine."

"Is that all?" laughed Spider. "Here, I'll take the first drink."

Spider took a small sip from the glass and then passed it on to Turtle. "No, my friend," protested Turtle, "you must drink the entire glass."

It was a big glass. By the time Spider finished it, he already wasn't thinking as clearly as he usually did. Turtle poured the host another glass and began to ask questions.

"Tell me, Spider, who else have you invited here to this wonderful tree?" When Spider mentioned his guests, Turtle noted that each of them was missing from the bush community. He questioned further, "And does anything unusual ever happen here?"

Spider only giggled and finished his palm wine. Turtle quickly filled the glass again.

"I'm curious, Spider. How can you make soup out here in the bush with only palm oil? What else do you put in the soup?"

By this point, Spider was completely drunk. He smiled at Turtle and said, "I'll show you the recipe for my special soup." He walked over to the palm tree and said, "First, I get plenty of palm wine, good fresh palm wine. Then, I mix it well with whatever guest I can find that day. When they are thoroughly blended, I stir them into the palm oil I have boiling over here. The guest is happy with his palm wine, and I'm happy with my soup. Everyone is happy!"

Spider staggered over to the pot. "I'm very happy," he declared as he took another drink of his palm wine.

"You're very drunk and very cruel," snapped the turtle. "How could you do this to the animals in our community?"

Spider shook his fist at Turtle and started to say something, but the words never came out. Before he had a chance to speak, the spider lost his balance and fell over backwards into his own cooking pot. Turtle returned to his chair with a his own glass. There was nothing he could do to save the last victim of the palm wine trap, but he could sample some of the fresh palm wine.

THE RULE ABOUT THE MOON AND STARS

Long ago when God first created people and put them in a village, the sun, moon and stars were very close to the earth. Back then nobody had to work under the hot sun. Whenever people were hungry, they simply cut off a piece of the moon or stars and ate as much as they wanted. There was plenty of time to enjoy life. Every day was like a holiday. Mothers took their children on long walks. Lovers strolled hand in hand. Fathers and sons spent their days with games and sports. Whenever anyone grew hungry, it was easy to slice off a refreshing piece of the moon. It always tasted just right.

"There is only one rule that must be followed," every father told his children. "God does not like waste."

"No waste at all?" nearly every child asked.

"That's right, my children. No part of the moon or stars can ever be kept overnight or thrown away."

"But what if someone cuts off too much?" was also asked by nearly every child.

"Everyone is free to cut off as much or as little as they want," they were told. "As long as everything is eaten by sunset, and nothing is wasted, all will be well."

"But, Father, what will happen if someone cuts off too much? What if some of the food is wasted?" These were often the last questions asked by all curious children.

"Nobody really knows," all fathers replied. "It's never been done before. We aren't really sure what will happen. But nobody I know is brave enough to break this rule. Are you?"

"No!" Absolutely every child who ever heard this story always said the same thing. Nobody wanted to break God's rule. Nobody was really that foolish.

But, there had to be a first person.

There always is.

Now, in one distant village, there lived a young woman who never liked to be told what to do, ever. She never liked to be told what to do as a child. And, that never changed. Even when she grew up and was married, when her husband told her to do something, she often did the exact opposite. That attitude didn't work well for her as a child. It really didn't work well for her as an adult. Still, she thought rules were made to be broken. All rules. She even felt this way about the rule concerning how much of the moon and stars could be cut.

She never actually broke that rule, but she had considered it for a very long time. It wasn't a wise thing to consider. That didn't stop her from thinking about it.

Once, when her husband was gone all day, the wife decided to see just what would happen if the rule were broken. "Was it really all that serious?" she wondered.

She found a ladder and gathered her children to help her. She speedily cut out chunks of the moon as the children gathered slivers from the stars. Once the children realized they had enough food for the day, they quit their work. However, their mother urged them on. "This food is so very sweet," she said. "Let's see how much we can gather this morning."

"But, Mama, we've always been told by Papa that we are not allowed to waste any food."

"I know he says that, but what will happen if we do it just this one time?"

"Nobody knows the answer, Mama. And, nobody wants to know the answer either," the children warned.

In spite of their cries, the wife spent all morning cutting out chunks of the moon and slivers from the stars. She worked rapidly and cut out an enormous amount of food. Then, she and her children relaxed the rest of the day, casually sampling the delicious foods.

When the husband came home and saw what his wife had done, he was vexed! "You foolish woman! What have you done?" he cried. "We can't possibly eat all of this food! You will bring trouble upon us all with your foolishness."

The woman wasn't as concerned about the rule as much as she worried about her husband's anger. Immediately, she started eating quickly. The children and husband did the same. But it was obvious there was too much food for one family.

"It's getting late, and the sun is going down!" said the husband. "We must ask the rest of the villagers to help us."

The cry for help was sent out and the villagers came. They came, young and old, men and women, as well as all of the children. Everyone wanted to help but it was already too late in the day. Most of the villagers had eaten supper, and they were already very full. Everyone tried to eat quickly, but there was just too much to eat.

And then, the sun went down.

As darkness settled upon the village, a hush grew over the crowd.

A woman cried out, "The rule had been broken."

Another small child joined her and asked, "What is going to happen to us?"

They soon found out.

With a clap of thunder and a burst of lightning, God appeared before the villagers. His voice boomed, "You could not be satisfied with what I provided for you! Today you have broken my rule and wasted my blessings!"

"It was her!" declared the husband, pointing at his wife. And, there was no confusion about who the guilty woman was. Everyone else also pointed at her as well.

"You were all warned. It doesn't matter who broke the rule," declared God. And then, He banished the sun, moon and stars from the presence of the villagers. No longer would they be within man's easy reach. They were cast to the far corners of the sky. From that time unto now, man has had to work for his food. And unfortunately, people are very slow to learn their lessons. Many children still hate to be told what to do.

Are you one of them?

THE TREASURE CAVE

"I've found a cave filled with treasure," announced Opossum. "Although somebody lives in the cave, there doesn't seem to be anyone around there today. I think we should go help ourselves to some of the riches."

"We would have to be careful," cautioned Cockroach. "We would be in big trouble if we were caught stealing."

"I think I have a solution," Boa Constrictor said with a smile. "Let's invite Spider along. After we take some treasures, we can tie Spider up and leave him. He'll be in trouble for stealing, and we'll have time to take the riches far away from the cave."

The three friends agreed on this plan. Spider, though suspicious of their invitation, was not able to pass up their offer. They set off for the treasure cave wondering just what this adventure would bring them.

The cave was exactly as Opossum had described. Nobody seemed to be at home that day, and the place was filled with treasures. "This is better than I ever expected!" cried Cockroach as he headed for the boxes of riches. "Wait for a second," hissed Boa Constrictor. "Isn't there something we must do before we remove any of these treasures?"

Boa circled Spider with a wicked grin, and Spider realized he was in serious trouble. He wasn't sure exactly what the three had in mind, but he knew it was not in his best interest. Opossum, with a rope in his hands, joined Boa. Cockroach, however, was not to be distracted by the situation with Spider. There were treasures to be had, and Cockroach had to have them.

Although the four animals were unaware of it, the cave was very well protected, and they were not going to be leaving with any treasures. The owners of the cave placed some magic on the riches. If anyone tried to steal anything, a spell would close the entrance of the cave.

There would be no escape. Anyone caught would be trapped until the owners of the cave returned.

Darkness surrounded the animals the moment Cockroach lifted the first box of riches. The cave door sealed shut.

"What happened?" shouted Boa.

"The cave door shut!" cried Opossum. "We're trapped."

"How are we going to get out of here?" wailed Cockroach. "We'll be captured as soon as the owners return."

Only Spider remained calm. The three other animals, who had planned to treat him so poorly, turned to him for help. "Where can we hide?" they pleaded. "You are the clever one here. Tell us what you think we should do."

Spider was indeed clever - but he wasn't very forgiving. He was not about to help the three animals who planned to harm him. He suggested places for the trio to hide - but the locations were not safe havens. They were traps!

"Boa, you should go hide among the firewood," instructed Spider. "Wrap yourself around the logs and remain very quiet."

The snake slithered into position.

"Opossum, you should go to the rice bag," suggested Spider. "Burrow down deep into it and do not move."

The opossum did as he was told.

"Finally, Cockroach, I think you should hide in the oil jar," advised Spider. "Be careful to place the lid back on carefully."

After Cockroach slipped into the oil jar, Spider silently crept up the wall to a far back corner of the cave. It was quiet and dark. Spider calmly awaited the return of the owners. He didn't have to wait long.

A loud noise alerted the animals when the cave door opened.

The animals held their breath in fear when they heard a booming voice, "Who would dare enter my cave? Whoever has come here will not leave. I will have them for my soup!"

The owner of the treasures ordered his wife to start preparing the soup while he and his sons searched the cave for the intruders.

The woman grabbed her cooking pot and went to the firewood pile. "Husband!" she screamed. "The intruder is here in the firewood. Come and get him."

Boa Constrictor was so tangled in the firewood that he had no chance of escape. The owner of the cave quickly killed him with his cutlass. With a huge grin, the man declared, "We'll have fine meat for our soup now."

The woman continued preparing her meal. When she reached for her oil, she found Cockroach floating in the jar. He had drowned. "Husband," she cried, "there was a second intruder. Get rid of this dead cockroach. He's not going in my soup."

As the soup boiled, the woman reached for her rice bag. She noticed the tip of Opossum's tail in the rice. "Husband," she called, "our soup will be very good tonight. I have found a third intruder."

Opossum was trapped deep inside the rice bag. There was no way for him to escape. The husband came back to the kitchen with his cutlass and killed the opossum. Immediately, the old woman added the meat to the soup.

The kitchen smelled wonderful. The aroma filled the cave all the way to the back corner where Spider remained hidden. It wasn't long before the family settled down for a fine meal of rice and soup. As they hungrily ate the feast, no one noticed as Spider quietly crept along the ceiling of the cave and outside to freedom.

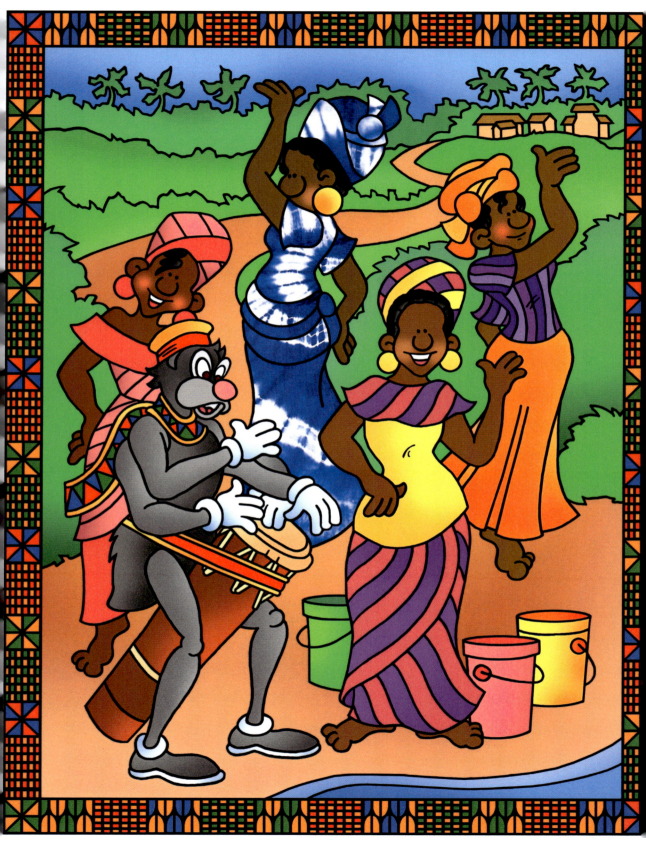

A GRACIOUS HOST

"I know that I'm going to a feast held in my honor," thought Leopard, "but I am just too hungry at this very moment. I cannot wait until I arrive at that distant village. I must have something now. I think I'll stop here at this house and visit my friend. If I am lucky, he will offer me a little food. At least, I sure hope he will."

Unfortunately for Leopard, that particular house belonged to Spider. Everyone knew about Spider and his food. He never shared anything with anyone. Absolutely never. It wasn't going to happen. As soon as Leopard sat down on the front porch, he could smell the yams that Spider was roasting over the fire behind his house. A bowl of hot yams was exactly what Leopard needed to satisfy his hunger. Immediately, his mouth started to water.

Of course, Spider greeted his guest politely. The two friends had not seen each other for a while, so there was a lot to catch up on. But, friend or no friend, Spider had no intention of sharing even one yam. Leopard, on the other hand, was determined to give his friend every possible chance to share his food. When Leopard realized that Spider really wouldn't share anything, he was vexed. And, the vexed leopard had a plan to punish Spider for his selfishness.

Spider wouldn't eat the yams as long as Leopard was at his home. Leopard knew that, so he continued talking while the yams roasted behind the house. Leopard didn't stop talking until the yams were nothing but black ashes.

"I see it is getting late and I don't want to travel after dark. I must go now," apologized Leopard, after he was certain all of the yams were ruined. "Do you know there is a feast in the village tomorrow? It is in my honor. I do hope you will join us."

"Oh, I'll be there," promised Spider. What he didn't say was that he already planned a way to get even with Leopard for spoiling his meal. "You can count on my attendance."

"Excellent, my friend," replied Leopard. Then, he continued down the path to the village.

Spider indeed came to the village the following day, but he didn't enter the celebration. He remained hidden in the bushes as he watched the day's activities.

Finally, the moment arrived that he had been waiting for. "The food is starting to boil," he noted. "And just about now, the women cooking the meal are going to need some more water. It's time I move into action and teach that leopard a lesson."

Grabbing his drum, Spider rushed down to the stream where he knew the women gathered water. He set up his drum and began beating a rhythm. Now Spider was very talented. Just imagine all his many arms pounding on the drum!

As a few women approached the stream, they heard the beat. And, they liked what they heard.

"Who's got a drum? I didn't hear anything like this back at the village celebration," said the first woman.

"I don't know who's doing this either," said another woman, "but it's making me want to dance."

When the women arrived at the edge of the stream, they saw the musician.

"Spider, we should have known it was you with your drum," declared the chief's wife.

As the women placed down their empty containers, one woman looked at Spider and said, "You know there is just no way that we can resist the beat of your music."

Spider just smiled at them. He knew this all along. And, that's exactly why he brought his drum to the stream. He continued his beat while the women swayed to its rhythm.

As more and more women came to the stream for water, the area became more and more crowded. And, every woman who heard Spider's music placed her water container aside and joined in on the dance.

Spider's smile just widened. With so many arms and legs, he could beat his drums as long as he wanted. And, he wanted all those women to enjoy his talents for as long as they wanted to dance. Eventually, all of the women in the village came to the stream, every one of them singing and dancing.

Spider had a wonderful time.

He also had his revenge on Leopard, just as he planned all along. As the women enjoyed his music, he knew all of their food back at the village celebration continued to boil away. And if they danced long enough - and he knew they would - all those bowls of palm butter, potato greens and cassava leaves would burn as black as his yams.

It took a while for the men in the village to notice that all of the women were missing. It didn't happen until one man got so hungry that he had to check on the cooks. By the time he noticed that all the women were missing, it was too late to save any of the food.

"My friends," he declared to all the men, "something is up. I'm not sure what it is, but there is not a single woman left in our village. The food is all burned beyond saving and the women are all gone."

"No food?" asked nearly every man present.

"What are you talking about?" demanded the chief.

"It's exactly what I said," the man replied. "They are all gone."

That news stopped all conversation. And when there was complete silence, they also heard the distant drum beat.

"I think that drum might have something to do with this," said the chief.

So, all of the men set out to follow that beat and find what happened to their women. Of course, their search finally led them to the stream. When they saw the dancing, the men also forgot about the feast and joined in the new celebration.

Leopard was the last to locate the villagers. Their laughter directed him to the stream. The music was so good, and he could see the people were having a fine time. However, he was determined not to be the same kind of host that Spider had been. Before joining in the dancing, Leopard returned to the village to get Spider a plate of food. He returned with a heaping bowl of black cassava leaves and burned rice.

"My friend," he said with a chuckle, "you didn't feed me yesterday, but I want to be a more gracious host."

Spider laughed and played his drum all the harder as Leopard joined in the dance.

RED DEER'S SECRET MISSION

"This is getting serious," cried Leopard. "How does that hunter always seem to find us?"

"No matter how deep into the bush we go, that man knows where we are hiding," wailed Monkey.

"I suspect he has some kind of special magic," said Red Deer. "It must be very powerful."

"We have to call all the animals together and decide what to do about this man," declared Elephant. "Let's meet tonight behind the big tree."

Most of the animals in the bush gathered that night to discuss their concerns about the mysterious hunter. There were several suggestions.

Turtle said, "Let's just ignore the man. He'll eventually go away anyway."

Nobody liked that idea. No one really thought the man would ever go away. They knew Turtle wasn't worried because he had a protective shell.

"I think the man should be eaten," suggested Leopard.

"That's not a bad idea," replied Monkey, "but there are always more of them coming. I suggest we move to another spot deep in the bush where people rarely ever go."

Finally, it was Red Deer who came up with the idea that everyone could agree upon as their best option. "I can turn myself into a human being and visit the hunter in his village," she said. "As a lovely young woman, I may be able to solve this problem that none of us as animals can understand. Hopefully, I can learn this man's secret for being such a skillful hunter."

It was a matter of life and death for the bush animals. So, it was agreed that Red Deer should go as soon as possible. Red Deer said she would go to the village the following day.

It caused no small stir when a beautiful, unknown woman entered the village. The man was so very pleased when he heard this woman say, "I'm looking for the great hunter." He had no idea that his reputation as a hunter went beyond his village.

"Oh, my hunter," whispered Red Deer, "I live in a distant part of the bush. Word has reached far and near of your skill as a hunter. You are indeed a great mystery. That's why I have come. I just had to see this great hunter for myself."

"It's really no great mystery," confessed the hunter. "The secret to my successful hunting is the magic found in this small bag that I have right here on the table. I always carry it with me when I hunt. In the two months that I have owned it, I have become the greatest hunter in my village."

"Not just in this village, but you have become the greatest hunter in the entire bush," declared Red Deer.

The hunter smiled at the praise.

He enjoyed the attention from such a beautiful woman. And, he had no idea what was really on Red Deer's mind. She planned to steal the bag of magic. In fact, she planned to steal it at the very first possible chance she found. And, the opportunity came very soon!

There was a knock at the hunter's door.

"Who could that possibly be right now?" thought the hunter. "And, what rotten timing! Don't they know at this very moment that I am with a very beautiful woman?"

Certainly, most people in the village were aware of that. It didn't take any time for that word to spread. But, someone from a neighboring village wanted to know if he had any fresh meat to sell.

Of course, he did. He was the great hunter. While the man took care of the sale, Red Deer saw her opportunity. She quickly stole the magic bag from the table top and quietly slipped out the hunter's back door. She dashed into the bush and raced back to the assembly of animals at the big tree.

There was complete silence as Red Deer told of what she had learned in the hunter's village. "It's this little bag," she explained as she lifted it above her head. "It contains special magic that he used to hunt us. But, he no longer owns it!"

There was a cry of joy among all of the animals. Red Deer was their hero who saved them. And soon, there was loud celebrating with plenty of dancing. The celebrating lasted long into the night.

Meanwhile, back in the village, the hunter quickly realized that the lovely woman actually had no interest in him. It had all been a lie. She had only come to steal his bag of magic. "But, why would she do it?" he wondered.

"She must somehow be an animal in human form," an old woman in the village declared. "She did this to stop our greatest hunter and her biggest enemy."

The hunter was vexed. "I can't believe that I was so easily tricked by a beautiful woman's words of praise!" He grabbed his gun and headed into the bush.

Many other men of the village joined him. That night, it didn't take any magic to find the animals. The noise of their celebration echoed throughout the bush. The hunter and other villagers quietly crept up on the joyous animals. The villagers completely surrounded their unsuspecting targets. The surprise attack ended the celebration abruptly and left several animals dead or wounded. In the confusion, Red Deer escaped with the bag of magic, but many of her friends were left behind dead.

Since man lost the magic bag that night, he has had to rely on his skill and cunning to hunt for his food. The animals, too, learned a lesson from that evening. Never again will they all assemble in one location for loud celebrating. Instead, most animals generally speak in whispers. They don't want Man to find them. And, they certainly don't want him to know the mysteries of the bush. Their greatest secret is still the location of the magic bag that Red Deer stole. She has hidden it very well.

THE HOUSE THAT SPIDER BUILT

"Aren't you ever going to finish your house, Spider?" asked Elephant. "I thought when you plastered the walls that you would be finished, but then you made a fence. After that you planted flowers. Then, you painted the house. Next, you added rogue bars and screens. It seems like you are always finding things to do to your house when it looked fine long ago."

It was true that Spider built a fine house. He took great pride in knowing it was the nicest house in the village. He enjoyed the attention of his neighbors. He liked the questions from Elephant and the others.

"My dear Elephant," replied Spider, "there are only a few more things to add to the house. It is nearly completed."

But really, there were a lot more improvements that Spider planned. He added a front and a back porch. He made shelves for the kitchen. He even made an indoor bathroom! The neighbors continued to marvel. There just didn't seem to be an end to the things Spider wanted for this house!

Instead of the usual thatch, Spider added zinc sheets for the roof. It was the only house in the village with a zinc roof. This made Spider nearly burst with pride. The final thing that Spider built was a palaver hut right next to the house. He planned to enjoy the cool breezes of the evening relaxing in a hammock inside the hut. He quickly, but skillfully, built the hut and personally added the thatch leaves for the roof. He was so anxious to have everything finally completed. On the first evening when his home was finished, Spider lit candles in the palaver hut and waited for his friends to come admire his work. Elephant was the first neighbor to visit and he squealed, "Everything is so very perfect!" Everyone else agreed.

Spider basked in the approval of his neighbors. Some brought rice dishes in addition to the kola nut and palm wine that Spider provided. It was an evening filled with celebrating and dancing around the palaver hut. When everyone finally left, Spider sat back in his hammock and grinned. He had so very much to be proud of. He fell asleep very contented.

Now, you know how the story ends. As Spider slept, a gentle breeze blew the flames into the thatch roof which, of course, caught on fire. With amazing speed, the inferno spread to the brand-new house. By the time Spider awoke, it was too late to save anything. His pride turned to despair as surely as his possessions turned to ashes. But, in this village, Spider had many friends. They took him into their homes while he rebuilt. He was well-cared-for until he completed a much simpler home.

THE SCHOOL WHERE NOTHING WAS LEARNED

"Our school building is now completed, and the teacher has arrived in town," announced Hog. "Now we can start classes and begin our education."

The teacher knew what should be taught in the school, but the animals of the town had ideas of their own.

Hog said," One period every day should emphasize eating. Oh, yes, maybe even two!"

On the other hand, Rabbit suggested, "We must study hopping. How else are we going to get anywhere?"

"The answer to that is simple," replied Hawk. "We all need to study flying."

Of course, Squirrel knew they were all a little crazy. He insisted, "There should be classes on climbing trees. It's the most important thing to be taught."

The new teacher simply shook his head. "These animals only want to study what they can already do very well. How much will they really learn?"

The first day of classes arrived, and the teacher and his four students all came to school early. "The first period's lesson will be eating," said the teacher.

"That's exactly what I wanted to hear," cried Hog. Of course, he needed no instructions. He ate and ate and then ate some more. He ate so much that it made the other animals sick.

"There is no way I can possibly eat anything after what I just witnessed," cried Rabbit. And, the other animals felt about the same. Nobody had the stomach to eat after watching hog take his turn. Naturally, Hog passed the lesson in eating easily while everyone else failed miserably.

"Okay, students, I think we can move on to our second lesson of the day," declared the teacher. "And now, we're going to focus our attention on hopping."

"Thank goodness!" sighed Rabbit. This time it was Rabbit's turn to shine.

"Look at him race through the course that the teacher prepared," said Hawk.

When he had finished the course, Rabbit asked, "Can I do it all over again?"

"He can sure do it for me," said Hog with a burp. "I just ate, and I'd gladly have a little more dessert, but I'm not about to run, hop or move after my meal."

The other animals were unable to complete their hopping assignment. Nobody except Rabbit felt any kind of success during the period.

"We're ready for period three, students," announced the teacher. "It's time to fly."

After two periods of failure, Hawk was ready for this lesson. "Finally," he declared, "there is something in this school that I can do well. He flapped his mighty wings, lifted off the ground, soared through the air, and left his fellow students in his dust. He made sweeping dives around the school and then gracefully landed in front of the other classmates. Naturally, no one else was able to get up off the ground. Hog mumbled something about, "When pigs fly . . . "

"For our final period of the day, we'll study climbing," said the teacher with a smile.

Before he could give any instructions, the squirrel scampered off. "Finally!" he cried as he raced up a tree and out of sight among the branches.

The teacher knew that Squirrel was anxious to do something well after a very long day of school. But he could also see frustration in the eyes of all the other animals. They each knew that they could not do this task. As Squirrel scampered up and down several trees, the other animals simply sat down in complete frustration.

"If you just asked me to fly up to the uppermost branch, I'd pass this class," mumbled Hawk.

"And I could run circles around the tree if you'd like," said Rabbit.

"As for me, I'd still just like to sit if you don't mind," replied Hog. "It wasn't that long ago that I ate."

When Squirrel scurried back to the group, the teacher said, "I think this first day of school wasn't exactly what you had expected it to be. Each of you miserably failed three of your four classes."

The students looked down at their feet, or claws or paws. They knew their teacher was right.

"Yes, I can see that nobody succeeded much in school today," continued the teacher. "All you have managed to do is show me what everyone already knew you could do well. What did you learn today?"

The four students hung their heads a little lower in shame. For a long time, it was completely silent. Finally, Hog said, "I don't think we learned anything."

"Well, I think you all should have learned one very important lesson," declared the teacher with a smile. "You should have realized that the reason you come to school is to learn. There are some things we can learn and some things we cannot learn. Tomorrow we will begin lessons that each of you can learn. I will teach you the things that I came here to teach you."

The four students left school that day knowing that they had a very wise teacher. Tomorrow their classes would begin, and they would be ready. But the animals knew their education had already begun.

WHY CROCODILES AND HUMANS CANNOT BE FRIENDS

Sometimes the old crocodile enjoyed it when the little boy from the village walked on his back. It relieved his itch like nothing else he knew. But there were other times, other times when the child angered the old crocodile. When the boy's shoes had small rocks caught in them, they really hurt the crocodile's back. On other occasions, the boy's fishing hooks caught in his tough skin. Of course, the small boy never realized it was a crocodile he stood upon each time he went to the river. The crocodile always rested in the same position. The boy simply thought it was a big, green log to climb upon. It was indeed his favorite "log" along the river.

Now, this was an old crocodile. He expected to receive a certain amount of respect for his age from anyone and everyone younger. He felt no respect at all when the young boy tried to sharpen a knife on his tail. The old animal's anger flared up inside him. "How was it possible for a young boy to treat me so rudely?" he thought. It was such a lack of respect! On that occasion, he nearly ate the child on the spot. With a little flick of his tail and a snap of his jaws, the problem with respect would suddenly resolve itself.

But he didn't do that.

Instead, the old crocodile called his family and friends together. Everyone agreed that the boy behaved poorly. Some of the older crocs urged their friend to eat the boy the next time it happened, even though crocodiles had never eaten humans before.

Finally, one crocodile stood up among the rest and calmed the others down. "I know this little boy," he explained. "His parents died last year, and each day he must beg for rice and find his own fish. I'm sure he doesn't even know he's offended you. Let me go to the human village and explain the problem. I'm sure we can solve this without violence."

All of the animals, even the old crocodile, agreed this was the wisest thing to do. The crocodile with the calming words dressed up like a human and set off for the village. He almost looked like a human except for his long, sharp teeth and tough, green skin.

When the peculiar stranger arrived in the village, everyone noticed him. His arms might have been a little short, and he may have spoken with a slightly unusual accent, but he also had plenty of palm wine and cane juice for the villagers. Everyone soon forgot that he was any different from them.

"On my way to the village," said the guest, "I saw many hundreds of crocodiles in the river. Although these animals are very beautiful, they are also stronger than elephants and faster than fish. It's a shame that their meat makes people sick."

None of the villagers knew anything about crocodile meat. They had never killed one before. But as the visitor spoke, the villagers certainly listened.

"Believe it or not, I can actually understand these crocodiles when they speak," announced the guest.

That announcement really impressed the people of the village.

"Did you know they are vexed with the small boy who comes to the river each day? Every day he fishes on top of an old crocodile, but he never shares anything with his host. It's just so very disrespectful. I suggest that you keep that small boy away from the river or there is a very good chance that he will be eaten."

After saying what needed to be said, the crocodile got up to leave. The villagers thanked him for his advice and assured him that they would keep the boy away from the river. When crocodile returned to his friends, he told them all about his experience. "The humans are not so bad," he admitted, "and they promised to keep the small boy away from the river."

Everyone was relieved.

Unfortunately, the villagers had enjoyed too much of their guest's palm wine and cane juice. In the morning, nobody remembered the warning. Much to the old crocodile's amazement, the small boy was again at the river. His shoes had a few more rocks stuck in them which really hurt the crocodile's back. This time the old animal had no patience at all for this nonsense. He flicked his tail. He snapped his jaws. And, he promptly ate the little boy. The only thing he didn't eat were the shoes with all those small rocks. They hurt his teeth.

It wasn't until that evening that the villagers missed the small boy.

"He never came for rice today," cried an old woman.

"I haven't seen him since he left for the river this morning," said one of the children.

The villagers searched the path to the river. When they reached the water's edge, a small girl found one of the boy's shoes. At that moment, everyone realized what had happened to the poor child.

The girl who found the shoe was angry. "Crocodiles are so mean and ugly. If I ever find one, I will gladly shoot it!"

This comment coming from such a young child made the old crocodile giggle from his hidden position along the river's edge. It was the wrong time to giggle. The men heard a noise and looked for its source. When they found the old crocodile, one of the men shot him. That night there was great feasting and celebrating in the village. That was the night that everyone learned that crocodile meat was indeed delicious.

Sadly, it was the last night of celebrating in the village for quite some time. Crocodiles crept to the village to capture the man who killed their old friend. The next day men went to the river hunting more crocodiles. The killings continued because once the chain of violence began, it was impossible to stop. Crocodiles and humans have remained enemies ever since.

CHAPTER 4

Deep in the Bush Where People Rarely Ever Go is a collection of three plays from West Africa. The story begins in the bush, or rain forest, where a grandmother and three grandchildren have taken a walk.

INTRODUCTION

The Cast of Family Members:

Grandmother, Grandchild 1, Grandchild 2, Grandchild 3

―――

Grandchild 2: Grandmother, what kind of tree is that?

Grandmother: It's a honey tree, my dear.

Grandchild 2: Why is it way out here?

Grandmother: Because it only grows deep in the bush, where people rarely ever go. Where people rarely ever go . . . whew! We have walked far today, and I'm tired. Let's sit down for a bit.

Grandchild 3: I have some fruit if you'd like some, Grandmother.

Grandmother: Thank you, my dear.

Grandchild 1: Give it to me!

Grandchild 3: Grandmother first, me second, and you . . . well, maybe.

Grandchild 2: And what about me?

Grandchild 1: No, what about me?

SPIDER AND THE HONEY TREE

The Cast of Characters:

Spider, Young Girl

Grandmother: Children, there is plenty of fruit and no reason to fight. Settle down now. This reminds me of a story about a very selfish Spider and a honey tree - maybe this very tree. This story happened so very long ago. There was once a young girl from a faraway village who had a special talent. She could find the very best food in the bush. Her oranges were just a little bit sweeter, her plums just a bit larger and her bananas had just a little more flavor. Everyone in the village wondered where she found such rare and delicious fruit.

Grandchild 3: Many people must have followed her into the bush to find those special fruits. Don't you agree, Grandmother?

Grandchild 2: That would make her very popular.

Grandchild 1: No way! I would keep all that delicious fruit for myself.

Grandchild 3: That's selfish.

Grandmother: Actually, it was her secret. One day a lazy spider decided to ask the young girl to help him find food. The spider was too lazy to work for himself and was sure he could trick the little girl into sharing her secrets.

Spider: Little girl, you find the best fruits of all. Won't you take me with you just this once into the bush to find some?

Young Girl: I don't know . . . I've never done that before.

Spider: I promise not to tell a soul. It would mean so much to this humble spider if you would show me just this one time.

Young Girl: Do you promise to keep my secrets?

Spider: You can trust me.

Young Girl: Well . . .

Spider: Pull - ease!

Young Girl: I suppose I can show you just once. What do you like to eat?

Spider: Well, I like plums, bananas and especially honey!

Young Girl: I think I can help you.

Spider: What luck! We better start now before she has a chance to change her mind.

Young Girl: Now you must follow me deep into the bush, where people rarely ever go.

Spider: No problem!

Young Girl: It's quite a long walk, but I think you will find it worth the effort. We're almost there. Yes, this plum tree does not have much fruit. Most people completely ignore it. But its fruit is the sweetest in all of the bush.

Grandmother: Now, Spider was just as greedy as he was lazy. As soon as the young girl showed him the secret plums on that little tree, Spider's eyes got very large, and his mouth started to water. Then, he pushed the little girl into the bushes. The spider climbed the plum tree and ate every one of the plums. He didn't even leave one for the little girl.

Young Girl: And, he didn't even say thank you.

Spider: (rubbing a very full belly) This is the best day of my life. I wonder if she is foolish enough to show me more treasures? Why, if I were in her place, I would never have shown anyone these hidden secrets. But, I'm not complaining about this - no, not at all. As long as she guides me to the food, I will continue to eat everything.

Oh, little girl, is there anything else in the bush that you would like to share with me?

Young Girl: Would you like some bananas now?

Spider: Absolutely! And, before she has a chance to change her mind, I better get over to her.

Young Girl: Spider, we really must continue onward. There are plenty of other places I want to take you before the sun goes down. We just need to travel a little further down this path, where people rarely ever go.

Spider: Lead the way, and I will gladly follow you.

Young Girl: It's just a little further this way. Just over here you will find a patch of the very best bananas.

Grandmother: Now you already know what happened. As soon as the young girl showed Spider the banana plant, Spider's eyes got very large, and his mouth started to water. Then, he pushed the little girl into the bushes. The spider climbed the banana plant and ate every one of the bananas. He didn't even leave one for the little girl.

Young Girl: And, he didn't even say thank you.

Spider: Yum . . . that was delicious! This is how every spider in my family should live. Ahhh! I just love eating the treasures of the bush. But, the day isn't yet over, so I could eat more. That won't be a problem either since this girl is so foolish. As long as she guides me, I will continue to eat all of her food.

Oh, little girl, is there anything else in the bush that you would like to share with me?

Young Girl: If you are not too full, I know where we could find some honey.

Spider: I'm coming! I'm coming! I'm coming as quick as I can so she will not change her mind! Besides, I'm never too full for honey. Hurry up! I haven't got all day!

Young Girl: Just follow me a little deeper in the bush, where people rarely ever go.

Spider: Honey, honey, HONEY. I can hardly wait.

Young Girl: Well, you don't have to wait any longer. We've arrived. Over there is a very special tree. Deep inside a small hole is the most delicious honey you will ever find. I hope the honey pleases you. It's the best I know of.

Grandmother: And once again, you already know what happened. As soon as the young girl mentioned the honey, Spider's eyes got very large, and his mouth started to water. Then, he pushed the little girl into the bushes. The spider climbed into the honey tree to eat all of that sweet golden honey. He didn't save one drop for the little girl.

Young Girl: And, he didn't even say thank you.

But, go on right ahead and eat what you want. Of course, you'll be pleased. You love honey, and you're just about to make every part of my plan work. You'll learn to say thank you and a whole lot more. Just you wait and see.

Spider: This is so delicious, a real meal for a very special Spider - like me! All this golden honey. Every drop just for me. Why should I ever share?

Young Girl: Everything should be just about ready.

Spider: This is how life must be in paradise. With any luck, she'll show me the way to some more delicious treats of the bush.

Now I wonder, oh, little girl, is there anything else in the bush that you would like to share with me?

Young Girl: If you are not too full, I could easily show you where some more fruit grows. But, you must hurry. I have to go home soon.

Spider: Of course, I'll hurry. I don't want her to change her mind!

I'll be right there. Ahhh, my stomach. I'm stuck! Help me, little girl, I'm caught in the honey tree!

Young Girl: You haven't eaten too much now have you? Come on down right away, I have to go home soon.

Spider: Please, young girl, help me! I have grown too large. I cannot get out of the tree. You wouldn't want to leave a poor, old, helpless Spider stuck in a tree, now would you?

Young Girl: You wouldn't be stuck if you hadn't been so selfish. Now it is time for you to learn a lesson about selfishness.

Spider: I'm sorry for what I did! Please call for help! Pull-ease!

Young Girl: You aren't sorry for what you did. You are only sorry you are caught in the tree.

Spider: No, you're wrong (with fingers crossed). How did she know that?

Why don't I learn? All that food was so good and tasty. Next time, I'll bring all the food home. There I won't get stuck. That little girl is right. I'm the foolish one, and she's not a so foolish after all.

ONCE UPON WEST AFRICA

Please call for help. I beg you! I'm trapped here, and we are so deep in the bush where people rarely ever go. Please do this for me and I promise to be a better spider.

Young Girl: Well, okay, are you ready, Spider? Cover your ears because I'm ready to call for help.

Spider: I'm ready!

Young Girl: (stage whisper) Help! Help! The foolish spider is caught inside the honey tree. Somebody come and help this greedy spider.

Spider: What? Help me? Nobody can hear your whispers! Help!

Young Girl: (still whispering) Somebody help this foolish spider. Help!

Grandmother: Of course, nobody could hear her whispers for help. And nobody could hear Spider's cries from deep inside the honey tree. They were too far in the bush, where people rarely ever go.

The little girl looked up at Spider and smiled. It was getting late, and she had to hurry home. However, she promised to show the spider where her special oranges grew the following day if he was interested. Of course, Spider never showed up. Nobody ever heard from him again.

Grandchild 1: Yes, that's the kind of ending I like in a story. And they don't all live happily ever after!

Grandmother: That isn't the only lesson I want you to get from the story. There is a lot more to learn.

Granddaughter, is something wrong?

BLACK SNAKE AND THE EGGS

The Cast of Characters:

Black Snake, Chicken, Rooster

As Grandmother finishes her story, Grandchild 2 fidgets around checking pockets and the area around the ground in search of something she lost.

Grandchild 2: Where's my earring! Grandma! Grandma! My earring!

Grandmother: What about your earring?

Grandchild 2: I lost my earring. What do I do?

Grandmother: Let's try to find it and everything will be okay. Come on, children, let's look for her earring.

Grandchild 3: I hope you know that I do not appreciate crawling around on my hands and knees looking for your missing earring.

Grandchild 1: Are you sure you even lost it? I don't see the other earring. Did you even put them on this morning?

Grandchild 2: Of course, I put them on. I think . . .

Grandchild 1: You think?

Grandmother: Maybe you better stop and think about this. Did you put on your earrings this morning?

Grandchild 2: I think I put them on. I know I was worried about losing them this morning.

Grandmother: You know, you remind me of a story my papa always told me when I worried too much. Some things are worth worrying about, and some things just aren't worth the effort. You need to know which is which and then take responsible action. It was a lesson that Chicken needed to learn as well.

Grandchild 2: Please, tell us the story.

Grandchild 3: If it keeps me off my knees looking for missing earrings, I want to hear it too.

Grandchild 1: I hope this story has a little more blood or violence. I don't think Spider learned his lesson well enough in the last one you told us.

Grandmother: I promise you that a lesson is learned very clearly at the end of this story. Now, Chicken was not the type of creature to remain calm about anything. If she was worried, everyone knew it, and one day, her screams shattered the peace of the bush.

Chicken: My eggs! One of my eggs is missing. Yesterday I had twelve eggs, and today there are only eleven.

Grandmother: As Chicken ran from her nest to find Rooster, she had no idea that she was about to lose more eggs. Just out of view from the nest the thief silently and patiently waited for Chicken to leave her nest. Black Snake crept slowly and quietly up to eggs, and then he quickly swallowed one. It slipped easily down his long neck and was crushed by the muscles in his throat.

Black Snake: Such a silly chicken to speak to Rooster and leave her nest unguarded. Little does she know that I was waiting to eat another one. This plan of mine has worked so well; it only requires a little patience. (Then he gulps another egg.) A simple plan with great results. I must compliment myself. Delicious! I'll be back later for another scrumptious egg, Chicken. Thank you for such a tasty meal.

(As Black Snake slithers away, the frantic Chicken begins her conversation with Rooster at the other side of the stage.)

Chicken: Help me, Rooster, someone has stolen one of my eggs! How could someone take one of my eggs?

Rooster: First you must be certain you have all the facts. Are you sure you counted correctly? Maybe you just thought you saw eleven eggs. Put on your glasses and count the eggs again.

Chicken: You know I can count. Come and see for yourself. How many eggs do you see in my nest?

(They return across the stage to the nest.)

Rooster: One, two, three. (He frowns and stops counting aloud.)

Chicken: Well, what's the matter now? Are you afraid to admit for once that you were wrong and I am right?

Rooster: No, Chicken, it's nothing like that at all. Something is very wrong here. I only count nine eggs.

Chicken: What? Nine eggs! What is happening? Who would do this to me?

Grandmother: The next few days were just terrible for Chicken. She constantly worried about her remaining eggs. If she went to get some food or check on her other chicks, no matter why she left, the same thing always happened. One or two eggs were missing each time she returned to her nest.

Grandchild 2: How absolutely horrible! I would be a nervous wreck if this happened to me!

Grandchild 1: We already know that.

Grandchild 3: But this time the chicken deserves to be a nervous wreck. What did she end up doing? Surely she came up with some kind of a plan.

ONCE UPON WEST AFRICA

Grandmother: Well, a plan was devised, but it wasn't Chicken who thought of it. Let me continue . . .

Chicken: Someone is watching me very closely and knows exactly where I am each moment. I only have three eggs left.

Rooster: I am not always very good at solving these kinds of problems. But, out of all the animals that I know of, I can think of just one. Who is the only animal we know that loves eggs?

Chicken: Who? Who can it be?

Rooster: Black Snake, the worst reptile of all! You didn't know? He is famous for being a sly thief who always gets away with his crimes.

Chicken: Well, I know of him, but how did he do it?

Rooster: He is known for his patience. He is willing to wait a long time because he thinks that your delicious eggs are worth it.

Chicken: Eeeew!

Rooster: And besides, who else could slither in and out of your nest without getting caught?

Chicken: All right, you're correct. I can't believe I didn't know. Oh no! I forgot! My eggs! I've been away from my eggs far too long. I have to hurry before he comes again.

Rooster: Hurry!

Chicken: (frantically runs to her nest and peers inside) Oh, no! It happened again. That horrible snake came again! Rooster! Come quickly! My nest has been robbed again! There's only one egg left. Rooster, come help me! What am I to do?

Rooster: (runs over to check the nest) That slithering snake! I feared this was going to happen.

Chicken: I feared it too! And now there's only one left. What should I do?

Rooster: You must guard this last egg. No matter what, stay here day and night. Don't leave for any reason. Black Snake will see you on guard and won't come for the last egg. In the meantime, we must plan a way to stop Black Snake. This problem will only continue if we do not settle it once and for all.

Chicken: True, but what can we possibly do to stop Black Snake? He is so clever that nobody has actually even seen him commit this crime. What could we ever do to catch him?

Rooster: I've got it! Yes, I know what to do. Say good-bye to all your troubles from that horrible thief!

Chicken: Well, go on. What is the plan?

Rooster: Let me just say that no more eggs will be sliding down Black Snake's throat only to be crushed by his muscles. Let me tell you more about the plan because there is much we must do to prepare.

Grandmother: Rooster led Chicken away from the nest to prepare for their plan to stop Black Snake. Everything was said in whispers because they didn't want the snake to be suspicious at all.

The next day Rooster and Chicken tried to act as if nothing unusual was in the works. Black Snake was not to know a deadly plan had been set. The snake watched for hours until Chicken finally left her nest briefly to talk to Rooster.

Chicken: Oh, Rooster, may I have a word with you?

Black Snake: Ahhh, the grand finale! How foolish that little chicken was to think she could protect her eggs from someone as wise as Black Snake. The last egg is awaiting me. I will miss these wonderful eggs, but the last must be the best.

ONCE UPON WEST AFRICA

This plan of mine has worked so well. Don't worry, little egg. I plan to eat a lot more of you in the future. So lovely! So perfect! So delicious! So stuck in my throat! Uh oh, I can't breathe! I can't get this egg out either!

Grandmother: He squeezed the egg as hard as his muscles could squeeze, but all attempts to remove the egg were futile. He knocked at it. If he had arms, I'm sure he would have tried to reach down his throat. But slowly, slowly, very slowly, in great pain, and with a little overacting, the snake gasped his last breath and died.

Grandchild 1: All right!

Rooster: Well, I hope he learned his lesson.

Chicken: Whether he did or not, I'm sure he won't be repeating his crime anymore.

Rooster: That's for sure. Do you think that he had the slightest idea why that egg didn't break?

Chicken: No clue at all. How could he possibly have known that the egg was . . . hard-boiled?

Grandchild 3: What? Hard-boiled? Who would do something like that?

Grandchild 2: Oh, why didn't they just paint a rock white?

Grandchild 1: What are you complaining about? This is my kind of ending. The lesson is crystal clear - you get what you deserve - with a little death and violence on the side.

Grandmother: Well, I was hoping you'd see a different lesson.

Grandchild 3: Like never put all your eggs in one basket?

Grandchild 2: Or, don't count your chickens before they hatch?

Grandchild 1: No, the lesson is more like:

Open your mouth and pass the gums

You swallow trouble, and more will come!

Grandchild 3: That's disgusting.

Grandchild 1: What do you know? You're only a girl.

Grandchild 2: You think you know everything.

Grandchild 1: Well, boys do! We grow up to be men who rule and make decisions.

Grandchild 3: But women are every bit as capable as men. I'll be able to do whatever I set my mind to do when I grow up.

Grandmother: Now, now, children. This reminds me of another story. It's about the paramount chief who thought he was wise - but he still learned a lesson. And just for you, my dear, this tale happens to be a love story.

Grandchild 1: Yuck!

Grandchild 2: Yeah, a story I don't have to worry about.

Grandchild 1: Not possible.

Grandmother: Grandson, the chief was a little like you because he was not always able to admit that maybe someone else could think of a better idea than he. In fact, the chief's greatest pleasure in life was having others bring their problems to him for his wise advice. Now this story begins as two men come before the chief with a problem only he can resolve.

THE PARAMOUNT CHIEF WHO WAS NO FOOL

The Cast of Characters:

Father/Old Man, Chief, Neighbor, Daughter/Wife, Sheep Herder 1, Sheep Herder 2, Goats, Sheep, Members of the Family

---

(Two shepherds enter before the paramount chief. They bow deeply.)

Old Man: Oh, please, great chief, help me settle this dispute. It has been troubling me for many long days.

Chief: I'm always pleased to help my people. What is on your mind? I have yet to have a problem presented that I cannot handle. I assure you that I will solve your problem. There is no one else as wise as I.

Old Man: I am a poor farmer and as humble as can be. Until recently, I had a few goats, but now, I have nothing . . . nothing at all. My neighbor has stolen my herd. I confronted him saying they were mine and asked him to return them, but he refused. Please speak to him. I am a poor old man and cannot convince him.

Chief: And you, what do you have to say about this? Did you take this man's goats?

Neighbor: Of course not! I am not a thief! I have always had many goats. My neighbor has never had any of his own. I do not know what he is talking about!

Chief: Do you have any witnesses that saw this man steal the goats? Do you have any records showing the number of goats you own?

(Both shepherds shake their heads no.)

Chief: This will not be an easy problem to settle. If there are no other witnesses, I will have to rely on my own wisdom. And, that is the kind of problem that I enjoy the most.

I have an idea!

My people, I have a question for both of you. Whoever can answer it successfully will be the owner of the goats. It is merely one simple question. Answer me this: What is the fastest thing in the world? Go, and do not return until you know the answer.

Neighbor: How will anyone ever answer a question like that correctly?

Old Man: I think I need to return home and speak to my daughter. She is a very wise woman.

ONCE UPON WEST AFRICA

Ahhh, Daughter, you are not only beautiful but so very clever. I come to you for your help.

Daughter: What is it, Father?

Old Man: The paramount chief has sent me away with a question that is unbearably hard to answer. I must get it right to get my goats back. Oh dear! What am I to do? He has asked what is the fastest thing in the world? It might be the fleet-footed cheetah, but then I think that it must be the eagle that swoops through the sky. It is impossible to know for sure. And, I will never get my goats back unless it can be answered correctly.

Daughter: Why, Father, the answer is so simple. It's . . .

Grandchild 1: A lizard! I know it has to be. Every time I try to catch one, it leaps out of my reach!

Grandchild 3: Don't be so silly. Your brain certainly isn't the fastest thing in the world.

Grandchild 1: If you are so smart, what do you think it is?

Grandchild 3: I don't know either.

Grandchild 1: That's a first.

Grandchild 2: How could anyone know? What will happen to the old man's goats?

Grandmother: Well, the next morning, the paramount chief was very surprised to see the old man return so soon.

Chief: Do you have an answer to my question so quickly?

Old Man: Yes, my chief, the question was not that difficult.

Chief: So tell me, what is the fastest thing in the world?

Old Man: Time. We never have enough of it. It always goes too fast. There is never enough time to do everything that we want to do.

Chief: What an amazing answer! Could I have come up with such a reply? (Immediately he was suspicious of the man.) Who gave you these words? Whose wise thoughts do you share with me?

Old Man: They are my own words, my own thoughts. The credit is due to none but myself.

Chief: If you do not tell the truth, I will punish you. You will regret for the rest of your life the words that you have just spoken.

Old Man: Please forgive me, my chief. I confess these are the words of my daughter. She is very wise.

Chief: She must be! I would like to meet her.

Old Man: As you wish.

Grandmother: The Old Man brought his daughter and presented her before the chief. The attraction was instant and obvious to all. If the chief was impressed with the daughter's wisdom, he was captivated by her beauty.

Chief: You are indeed a wise and lovely woman. I would be honored to have you as my wife.

Daughter: The honor is mine, my chief.

Chief: Everything in my house is yours. I only have one rule for you. You must never become involved with any of the problems that are brought before me by the villagers. My judgments and solutions are entirely mine. I want no one else to interfere. This is your first and final warning. If you break this rule, I will banish you from my house.

Daughter: (She says nothing but only smiles and bows before the chief.)

(Grandmother again speaks as actors get ready for a scene change.)

ONCE UPON WEST AFRICA

Grandmother: As the days, weeks and months passed, the chief helped his people with their problems. His wife was careful not to interfere with his tests and decisions. Usually, she agreed with his judgments, but she always remained silent. However, one day, two young shepherds came before the chief.

Grandchild 2: Something will go wrong.

All other family members: Shhh!

Sheep Herder 2: Chief! Chief! He claims that my one and only sheep is his.

Sheep Herder 1: I only claim the truth.

Sheep Herder 2: You may talk smoothly, but the sheep is still mine.

Sheep Herder 1: Why don't we let our noble chief decide for that is the reason why we came here.

Sheep Herder 2: Yes, we will see that the sheep is mine.

Chief: Stop this babble and listen to me. I have a task for you. Whoever passes my test will own the sheep.

Sheep Herder 1: And what is this great task you ask of us?

Chief: I will give each of you an egg. Whoever hatches a chicken from it by tomorrow will claim the sheep. Now go away and think about how you will accomplish the task.

(Shepherd 2 walks away very puzzled and wanders to the chief's garden area where the new wife is resting.)

Sheep Herder 2: Everyone knows that I really own that sheep. This other shepherd is only jealous and wants what is rightfully mine. He thinks so quickly and talks so smoothly that other people always notice him. I may sit in his shadow, but I know the truth. But how is the truth going to help me solve this impossible problem? How can anyone hatch an egg in just one day?

Grandmother: The shepherd had not realized that he had spoken aloud. He didn't notice the other person in the garden. And, as it turned out, the person was the chief's wife. The shepherd had wandered into the wife's favorite resting spot in the garden. The wife could see how the child was troubled, and her heart was moved. Although she knew she shouldn't do it, she asked . . .

Daughter: What's the matter, young shepherd? Why do you look so sad?

Shepherd 2: The chief has asked something from me that is impossible.

Daughter: And what is that, shepherd?

Shepherd 2: He wants me to hatch a chicken egg in one day. What shall I do? He asks the impossible! I will fail the test and lose my only sheep.

Daughter: (turns aside in deep thought) I could help this young shepherd, but to do it would break the only rule my husband has asked of me. Even though it would displease him, how could I possibly ignore a child's pain? What would my husband think? What would I think of myself? (She thinks, then turns to the shepherd and smiles.)

Shepherd 2: Why do you smile? There isn't anything worth smiling about? Are you making fun of my problems?

Daughter: Cheer up, young shepherd. There is a simple solution to your test. You only need to take some seed rice to the chief.

Shepherd 2: Rice? Seed rice!

Daughter: Yes, rice. Tell him to plant it today so that in the morning you will have rice to feed your chicken.

Shepherd 2: I don't understand. How can planted rice give me a chicken?

Daughter: The chief will see the wisdom of your words. He knows it is just as impossible in one day to grow rice from seed as it is to hatch a chicken from an egg. Give the rice to the chief and share these words. However, and do not forget this, you must not mention anything about my help.

Shepherd 2: Thank you so much. Count on me to keep the secret.

Daughter: You are welcome. Now be on your way.

(The shepherd races around the stage to find the chief.)

Shepherd 2: Great chief, I have the answer to your test!

Chief: So quickly? I thought it was rather difficult.

Shepherd 2: It was not so hard for me.

Chief: If that is so, then speak up.

Shepherd 2: Here, my chief. Take this seed rice and plant it today so that in the morning I will have rice to feed my chicken.

Chief: (deep in thought) Well, well . . . who gave you this seed rice? And who gave you these words? Whose thoughts do you share with me? These words are too wise for one so young.

Shepherd 2: They are my own words, my own thoughts. The credit is due to none but me.

Chief: If you do not tell the truth, I will punish you. You will regret for the rest of your life the words that you have just spoken.

Shepherd 2: Uhhh . . .

Chief: What do you say, shepherd?

Shepherd 2: Please forgive me, my chief. I confess these are the words of your wife. My chief, she knew you would understand the wisdom of their meaning.

Chief: She was quite right.

Shepherd 2: I'm sorry I talked to your wife. I hope I have not displeased you.

Chief: You have been foolish. However, I do not believe that my wife would have helped you if she didn't think you were the rightful owner. I will respect her insight and let you take your sheep.

Shepherd 2: Yes, great chief, and thank you for your understanding.

Chief: Take your sheep and go!

And now, I must take care of the matter with my wife. (He crosses the stage to confront his wife.) My wife, I have a serious matter to discuss with you.

Daughter: Yes?

Chief: You have done the worst of all possible deeds. You have broken the only rule I gave you. I believed in you and respected you as an obedient wife. Didn't you know all that I have is yours? Now you have thrown it all away. Was it hard for you to follow one rule? There was only one rule that I gave you, and you have broken it. Now you must leave. Go back to your father's home.

Daughter: As you wish, my husband, I understand. I will be of no more trouble for you. I only ask one more thing. Please allow me to prepare one final meal for you before I go.

Chief: Do as you please. Make whatever you want. Take whatever you want. Just be certain that you do not remain here tonight!

(The chief leaves and the daughter begins food preparation.)

Daughter: What was I supposed to do? I know I broke his rule but thinking about it, what else could I have done? Let a child suffer? No, I couldn't do that.

But if my husband is as wise as he thinks he is, he should know what a wise woman he has for a wife. Let me see. Yes, I have a plan to win him back, and a little palm wine should do the trick. Just you wait and see, husband. I've got you just exactly where I want you.

Grandmother: The wife set about to prepare a splendid meal. She knew all of the chief's favorite dishes - pepper soup, palm butter, beans gravy and potato greens. However, his favorite dish was cassava leaves and she knew just how he liked it. The wife ushered the chief into the meal and set about serving him a feast he would never forget. Cassava leaves, combined with a very generous supply of palm wine, helped the woman's plans to work like magic. It didn't take long for the very full chief to grow weary and settle down for a nap. And, as soon as that happened, the woman's family came to help her transport the chief back to her father's home. The chief had no idea what had happened to him. He slept soundly through the night, but in the morning, the chief awoke with a start!

Chief: Where am I? What am I doing here?

Daughter: Good morning, my chief. I hope you slept well.

Chief: Where am I? How did I get here?

Daughter: You are in my father's home.

Chief: What are you talking about? Explain yourself, wife. Why did you bring me here?

Daughter: I did what you told me to do, my chief. You said I could take anything I wanted from your house as long as I was gone by nightfall. There was only one thing I wanted from your home, you, so I took you.

Chief: You are indeed a wise woman. Return with me to our home. Only a fool would send a woman like you away.

Daughter: And you, my chief, are no fool.

Grandchild 1: That's it? They all live happily ever after? What kind of story is that?

Grandchild 3: It's called romance. Don't you know anything about love?

Grandchild 2: Well, I for one am so relieved. But what if she breaks her promise a second time?

Grandmother: I don't think we need to worry about that. What we need to worry about is getting home before it gets too dark outside. You don't want to hear my stories about the spirits that lurk in the bush after the sun goes down.

THE END

CHAPTER 5

LIBERIAN ENGLISH VOCABULARY WORDS

Bitter Ball - a vegetable similar to an egg plant but shaped like a tomato.

Bush - Liberians do not use the words "jungle" or "rain forest." Instead, they call it "the bush."

Brushing - cutting grass or weeds with a long knife or cutlass

Bug-a-Bugs - termites.

Cane Juice - an alcoholic drink made from distilled juice of sugar cane.

Cassava - a root from the cassava plant. It is used like a potato and can be prepared in a variety of ways which include roasting, boiling, frying and baking.

Cassava Leaves - a soup made from ground leaves of the cassava plant. It is eaten over rice.

Cassava Sticks - Cassava is planted by cutting stems from an existing plant and sticking them in the ground.

Country Cloth - a heavy, homemade, traditional cloth.

Country Medicine - a variety of medicines and potions believed to have powers in healing or performing magic.

Cutlass - a long knife like a machete.

Devil - a man believed to have special powers for good or evil. He is frequently seen at funerals and other special ceremonies.

Dry Season - the six months of the year from about November to April when little or no rain falls.

Dumboy - a food made from cassava. It is thick and eaten by hand. A pinch is pulled from dumboy and swirled in a soup. It is then swallowed rather than chewed.

Fufu - also food made from cassava. It is not as thick as dumboy. It looks like white dough. A soup is poured over it, and the fufu is eaten with a spoon. Just like dumboy, it is not chewed. It is always swallowed.

Genie - a magical being with special powers who didn't need a lantern. It isn't pronounced the same as Aladdin's friend. Instead of "GEE NEE" it is pronounced "GEE NI."

Humbug - to pester, bother and annoy.

Hunger Season - also referred to as the Hungry Season, the time between when last year's crop of rice is all eaten and the current year's harvest is ready to be eaten. Many people go hungry then because sometimes food is hard to find.

Jollof Rice - a rice dish with several types of meat cooked which could include goat, pork, fish, crab, shrimp or chicken.

Kola Nut - a nut usually presented during formal welcoming. It is very bitter.

Lappa - two yards of material.

Palaver - to argue.

Palm Butter - a soup made for rice. It is made from the oil of palm nuts. Palm butter usually has fish, meat and many vegetables included in the soup.

Palm Butter Sifter - Palm nuts are boiled and beaten to a pulp. Palm oil is squeezed from this pulp. A palm butter sifter is used to help strain the pulp from the palm oil.

Palm Nuts - nuts that grow on certain palm trees. The nuts are used to get palm oil which is used in several ways.

Palm Oil - a red oil squeezed from palm nuts which have been boiled and then beaten in a mortar with a pestle.

Palm Wine - a juice tapped from certain palm trees. It is drunk almost immediately after it is tapped because it quickly spoils.

Parking Station - a truck or bus station. It's the perfect description because you park yourself there for hours, waiting for a ride.

Plums - mangoes.

Potato Greens - a leaf that is used in cooking a soup dish with rice. The leaves are from the sweet potato plant.

Rainy Season - the six months of the year from about May to October when rains are very common throughout Liberia. Parts of the country get more than 200 inches (or 5000 mm) of rainfall a year.

Rogue - a thief.

Scratch - to prepare the soil for farming with a hoe.

Street Meat - grilled meat for sale by vendors along the side of the road or in the market place.

Sweet - a word that means delicious. It has nothing to do with sugar. Good meat is usually described as sweet.

Taboo - something you cannot do for any of a variety of reasons.

Vexed - Liberian English for angry. Liberians rarely say the words "mad" or "angry" because they are generally "vexed."